Tea with
Ms. Tanzania

Tea with Ms. Tanzania

A Novel

Fayyaz Vellani

THE RED SEA PRESS

Trenton | London | New Delhi | Cape Town | Nairobi | Addis Ababa | Asmara | Ibadan

THE RED SEA PRESS
541 West Ingham Avenue | Suite B
Trenton, New Jersey 08638

Book design: Dawid Kahts
Cover design: Ashraful Haque
Cover illustration: Tavia Nyong'o

Congress Cataloging-in-Publication Data may be obtained from the Library of Congress.

ISBNs: 9781569027844 (HB)
         9781569027851 (PB)

For my beautiful mother,
a woman of mystery,
originality, and integrity.

There is no time to waste.
We must either unite now or perish.

—Julius Nyerere

Prologue

ry the beloved country. Of course, Alan Paton was alluding to South Africa, while I am referring to Tanzania.

I love Africa. But wait, you say, "Africa is not a country!" I am aware of this, my beloved son. But ask yourself, why did Miriam Makeba entitle her seminal album *Mama Africa*? I know you will point out that Africa is a continent. And furthermore, you will censure me for presuming to meld together a plethora of cultures and landscapes into one behemoth: Africa the Great.

Let me explain. As you know, I was born in Dar es Salaam—meaning *abode of peace*—in what was then known as Tanganyika. How many people do you know who had the good fortune to be born in a place with such provenance? I am here to declare that Dar really did live up to its auspicious name. At least, it did for a while. Read on, Zain.

If it is not already obvious, I will state for the record that I love Tanzania. There are many reasons for this. Assuredly, everyone has heard of the world's tallest freestanding mountain, Kilimanjaro; and the world's largest crater, the Ngorongoro; and of the magnificent Serengeti National Park, replete with lions, zebras, elephants, and wildebeest; and of Tanzania's beautiful coastlines, and its rainforests. I have not even detailed the delights of Dar, with its elegant white buildings, iridescent bougainvillea, and delicious sea breezes. And the people—the warmest I have encountered anywhere in the world. So I do love Tanzania with all my heart, for all these reasons and many more.

Alas, the moment one hears these words emerge from *my* mouth—silhouetted in a crimson tinge of Yves Saint Laurent lipstick—and hears my clipped accent—whose received pronunciation suggests the mighty oak tree rather than the languorous acacia—and glances just below this crimson mouth to the string of Chanel pearls adorning my neck, the thoughts emerge: *privileged, colonizer, wealthy, educated. She loves Tanzania from a distance. She escaped.*

And yes, this is all true. My life is a result of my having been born in that beautiful place, at that fraught time, but I am not ashamed of it. How can anyone be responsible for the location of their birth?

Perhaps people in my station ought to be grateful for all the wonderful privileges that life has gifted them. And I am. You may go even further and say that people like me ought to give something back. Well, I am doing that, too, right here on these sheets of paper.

This story begins and ends with Africa. The continent is ensconced in my veins. Those of us who say that we love Africa do so because we love our countries of origin, no doubt. But this experience of love encapsulates something more powerful than mere patriotism.

Africa's ambit extends far beyond its borders; geography is immaterial. It is a prodigious place, a vast assemblage of people, landscapes, and nation-states. But those who inhabit these nation-states belong to something greater, still.

Were this not true, why would the continent share a national anthem? As a child, I grew up singing *God Bless Africa,* as *Mungu ibariki Afrika,* while Alan Paton would have sung the same tune, with the words, *Nkosi Sikelel' iAfrika.*

Africa lies at the core of my very being. This is my story of Africa, humble but heartfelt.

Chapter 1

London, 2011

It was the most frightening day of my life, son. Many more unsettling times lay ahead, but January 20, 1964, was the commencement of a long process of my life's unraveling. Living the way I did—going on jaunts and safaris, flitting about the continent as if it were my playground—I had been confronted with many disconcerting surprises.

Do you remember me telling you the story of the crocodiles on my honeymoon with your father? Well, that was nothing next to January 20, 1964—a date which has been emblazoned on my mind for all these decades.

I'm finally unburdening myself. I'm sorry that you don't want to have any association with me—ostensibly because you don't approve of my political views—but I hope you'll read this, regardless. Maybe you'll get the answers you've been seeking. Besides, don't you know it's ungracious to refuse a gift? If I did anything right as a mother, at the very least I surely must have taught you how to be gracious. Sad and beleaguered, though, I am, this is my most precious gift to you, Zain. After all, everyone deserves to know where they came from.

Now that you are reading this tale, you may ask yourself why I have written it. I have no grandchildren, no descendants upon whom to bequeath my Chanel frocks and my Dior handbags. No daughter, or even daughter-in-law, to inherit my jewels. It may surprise you to learn that I do care for your darling, Aliseeya. After all, I watched the two of you growing up, side by side.

Nevertheless, she is not my heiress. Like you, Aliseeya Justice is an only child and will inherit everything from her mother. Believe me, Zain, that Damaris Justice has been stockpiling her trinkets for as long as I've known her. Yes, Damaris will bequeath everything to Aliseeya. Jamaicans are just like us—they love gold. Oh, how I wish I'd had a daughter. Please do not be hurt by this revelation. It's just that I've decided to be entirely honest with you about everything.

In any case, my legacy is dependent on you—my clever, socialist son living on a journalist's wages in Glasgow. You might change your mind about socialism if you'll just read through to the end. But I'd better not goad you. I know how sensitive you are, with your perfect and correct views. Please, Zain, for the love of your late father—I am aware that the God racket never worked on you—do carry on reading. I need you to. My life depends on it.

Incidentally, the God racket never worked for me either, darling. As Jomo Kenyatta pointed out, the missionaries taught us to pray with closed eyes. When we'd opened them, the mzungus possessed the land, and we were left holding nothing but the Bible. Don't be surprised that I'm quoting Kenyatta, my precious lad. Your mother is a much more complicated creature than you might have originally reckoned. I'm not just the glamour dragon you make me out to be.

I understand African Nationalism more than you'll ever know. In fact, I was tangled up in it. It will all become clear if you keep reading. Speaking of Kenyatta, did you know that his descendants are living here in London? They're just on the other side of the river, and I'm not done with them yet.

Never mind that for now. I'm not trying to deny how you must be feeling at this moment. I understand, my son, that you will be cross with me for not having shared this with you until now, for you are a hoarder of everything—books, clothes, emotions, and memories—just like your dearly departed father. It is because I feel his loss so keenly that I want to document this *histoire*.

Your daddy and my late mother were the only other people who knew about this tale. And with both gone, it is as though my own life is slipping away. I am not being melodramatic, son. More than half of my life, in memory, has gone with your father having suddenly vacated it. That man remembered everything. But I am different. I do not even trust my own mind, so I must safeguard this story while I still can, Zain.

Do you understand? I wish you would try. You always had so much empathy for the downtrodden of the world, but not for your poor old mother. Not that I'm poor. Or old. Well, not *terribly* old. But I digress. Grief for a partner is different from your grief for your dear daddy, my love.

You have lost your father, someone you looked up to. But he equipped you for life. You can carry on living. I do not say this to detract from the acute pain I know you feel in your heart. The loss of your father is an important milestone in your life, but not a coda to it. When you lose a spouse, someone with whom you created a life, it is as though the universe is saying, *It's time to start closing shop.*

You're left behind, but somehow expected to live in only half the house you have occupied for almost your entire adult life.

I have no need start at the beginning of my life, darling, for all that precedes that fortuitous day in January 1964, you already know. You always collected and hoarded my precious stories with the keenness of a boy in a sweet shop—an indulgence your father and I discouraged and were glad you never took up, preserving your perfect teeth so that benevolent smile could beam. I could think about that smile forever, my dear lad. Children have that effect. They take up all the mental and emotional room you can possibly give. Nothing else matters.

Let me stop being an indulgent mother, and set out on the task at hand—telling you my tale of Tanzania. Besides, I sense that you don't care for me anymore. Not like you used to as a boy. But this is not admonishment. Even as I'm starting to lose my grip, I want to make my exit as gracious as possible, bestowing this final gift as your inheritance.

On that sunny morning in Dar es Salaam, the weather no different from the others that preceded it, Shabani, our domestic worker, came knocking at the front door of our end-of-terrace house in Upanga, at an unsociable hour. As my ma opened the door, Shabani blurted out in Swahili, "*Jambo, Memsahib. Habari mbaya. Sarikari matata, sarikari bonneka. Dada Gulinari apana shule, apana shule.*" (Good morning, madam. Bad news. Government mutiny, government chaos. Sister Gulnar must not go to school).

And with that brief, frenzied pronouncement, he ran off. His second, *apane shule* was his sternest effort to protect me from going out into the lawless streets, delivered firmly yet respectfully. After all, a domestic worker cannot shout at his employer, even when he is trying to save her life.

We later found out that it had been too unsafe for anyone to be about. Tanks lined the languid streets around Oyster Bay near the Indian Ocean, not far from where we lived in Upanga. Closer to the center of town, armed soldiers were ostentatiously patrolling Independence Avenue. Any revolutionary worth their salt will use tanks, of course. But these are largely showpieces. Not that I knew this at the time, mind you. In fact, I recoil when I think about my naiveté.

Yes, darling, coups are much about optics as they are about power. Just ask the Air Force officers who tried to overthrow Daniel arap Moi in neighboring Kenya—another beautiful country plagued with lingering colonial malaise. Now stay with me son, for I know I have never taken you to these magical places of which I speak.

I have seen some of the most wondrous sights in my beloved Tanzania, as well as in Kenya and Uganda. I have journeyed all over Africa. I am very sorry about not showing you where I grew up, but it was too painful. I can never return to that place. The minute my Roger Vivier pilgrim pumps touch the Tanzanian tarmac, they will have me. By the end of this story, you will know exactly what I mean.

Remember how I looked in those photo albums you used to pore over as a child, back when you were still in awe of me? Try to imagine your sweet, young mother—I was once quite a dish, you know!—as head teacher at the Aga Khan Primary School, responsible for hundreds of little ones, being told by Shabani that there was an army mutiny, and that I should not go to work. Later that day, and in the weeks that followed, we learned the full details of the saga. But on that morning, I hadn't a clue.

Apparently, the trouble had erupted before dawn. At 1:30 a.m. on Monday January 20, 1964, the soldiers of the First Battalion Tanganyika Rifles had sounded an alarm at the Colito Barracks, just outside Dar es Salaam city limits. They arrested all the European officers present in the division, who were both the object of their disdain and their greatest asset in the ensuing negotiations.

In addition to demanding a salary increase to the tune of 150 percent, the Rifles wanted a speedier process of Africanization. That is, the promotion of African soldiers and the removal of European ones. Africanization is a funny word, is it not? What would your beloved Karl Marx have to say about it? You're just like your father in your naiveté.

Whoopsie daisy, I don't know how that slipped out! I'm sorry. I didn't mean it, darling. You can believe what you want to. Sometimes I can't help myself. Just stay with me as I take you back to that steamy January morning.

In what seemed like a well-orchestrated plan, the mutineers spread out across Dar like leopards creeping in the night. It was as though they had planted themselves high up in the trees like those fearsome, murderous cats, and then suddenly descended en masse into the city, as if out of nowhere.

Their first stop was the White House, which we called *Ikulu*. The Brits—who built it in 1922—called it the State House. Already, cracks were beginning to display in the Rifles' well-engineered plan, for our President Julius Nyerere had slipped away, perhaps out of one of the many doors of that grand, hulking edifice.

Apparently, Emilo Charles Mzena, the director of intelligence, made his way to the State House during, or just before, the arrival of the soldiers' representatives. Now think of it, son. How could this man have been alerted to the mutineers' whereabouts *and* have outsmarted them in the execution of their own plan?

Perhaps someone from within the ranks of the Tanganyika Rifles was disloyal and secretly wanted the mutiny to fail, so as to strengthen his own position in the army. History rests on the whims of turncoats. You think you can trust people, but I'm telling you, Zain, you cannot trust anyone. And that is partly why I am telling you all of this: they are after me.

Mzena managed to get some of his men to distract the soldiers' representatives, and he snuck President Nyerere out, to be taken into safe haven in a Catholic church—or so we would later hear. The Rifles must have realized that their plan was doomed within the first few hours, for everyone knows that if you want to overthrow a government, you must start at the top. Otherwise, your coup has no legitimacy. Never underestimate the importance of a figurehead. After all, everybody needs someone to look up to, and Nyerere had built a wellspring of reserve among the people of his beloved Tanzania.

On that January day, it seemed that Nyerere's egalitarian ways—even if noble and inspired by Mao Tse Tung—were not appreciated by all. He was another naive idealist, just like you and your father. By all accounts, Nyerere was an intelligent, benevolent man, though I never met him in person. I did meet his wife, Mrs. Nyerere, but I am getting ahead of myself.

What had particularly irked the Tanganyika Rifles was the suggestion by Mwalimu Nyerere—that was our Swahili honorific for him, meaning *teacher*—that the newly formed nation should be reasonable and sensible in its dealings with its non-African citizens. President Nyerere argued that the pace of Africanization should be slowed. After all, Tanzania had won her independence from Britain not even three years prior, and he was loath to take the country in what he saw as a backward direction.

But then he would, wouldn't he, sitting cozily in his sea-breezed rooms in the magnificent Ikulu? The specter of Tanzania's reputation plunging among the community of nations dismayed Julius Nyerere, that genteel graduate of Edinburgh University. The ever-present tug of war between being true to one's culture and succumbing to Western notions of progress loomed large over Nyerere. He was more of a Gandhi than a Guevara.

I know what you are thinking, Zain. By failing to capture Nyerere, the mutineers' hopes must have been dashed. The government's strategy of concealment worked so seamlessly that some speculated that the cabinet might have been tipped off before the mutiny had even begun. Was this the work of a disloyal Rifles soldier? Or could someone from within the government have been in cahoots with the mutineers?

Either way, our beloved Tanzania was never to recover from this event. Nyerere called it a national shame. He really played the part of a pedantic schoolteacher—the father of the nation berating his children for their foolish behavior. More mortifying than anything for the president was that he had been forced to go begging to our former British overlords for military assistance, forever undermining his personal and national sense of pride, and showing the world who really pulled the strings.

You see, son, pride of any kind is a precarious thing, and national pride can be an especially prickly beast. Pride is a false friend—fooling you into thinking yourself invincible when you possess it, and making you feel powerless when you lose it.

Tanzanians were both grateful and resentful toward Britain. After our independence, this delicate balance had tipped, ever so gently, into full-blown resentment.

To be honest, the Brits were an easy target. For one thing, they are not the friendliest people, are they? I say this as someone who has now lived in the United Kingdom for more than half of my life. Yes, they did liberate us from the Germans during the first World War, but they are still not the easiest people to get on with. Indigenous Tanzanians always felt that the British treated their country like a bank account. Let's face it, no one is sentimental about a bank account; one just withdraws what one needs.

As someone who has worked as a teacher with many Brits, both in Tanzania and here in London, I can attest that their approach to education—like their approach to life—can be imperious. Back in Dar, we always got the feeling that our British teachers used the educational system to rub our noses in how backward we were.

Yes, I gained a love of Dickens and Shakespeare from them, but implicit in these lessons was the understanding that we would never count ourselves among their number. We were simply a bank account being taught to speak the language of the account holder.

Chapter 2

L ater that morning, President Nyerere's whereabouts were unknown, not only to the mutineers, but even to his cabinet. Rightly, Nyerere trusted no one. Clever man. Secretly lurking in a hiding place of his own was Vice President Rashidi Kawaka, whom some suspected of being behind the mutiny. The president was well-concealed, as were all other cabinet ministers. All except for Defense Minister Kambona.

Oscar Kambona was a man to be reckoned with. Tall, handsome, articulate—he was proof positive of the power of appearances. I'm always telling you, Zain, keep your hair trim, iron your shirts, shine your shoes. Why can't you wear the Gucci horsebit loafers I bought for your twenty-fifth birthday, instead of those awful vegan clogs? People will respect you more, even in your left-wing world. For nothing impresses a socialist more than a soupcon of old money.

Won't you listen to your dotty old mum? You know I'm only thinking of you when I make such suggestions. A little fashionability never hurt anyone, son. But I am digressing, as my mind is wont to do these days.

Back to the mutiny. Kambona looked the part of strong leader. His haircut—parted on the left, just so—was the external manifestation of his fearless approach to life. Kambona wore his confidence like a second skin. Though he had hitherto been regarded as President Nyerere's sidekick, their relationship was never the same after January 1964. Just as Tanzania itself was never the same, and nor was your dishy mother.

Kambona taught me about how one person can have many faces. It was a necessary lesson, but one I wish I had never needed to learn. If my life is an elaborate quilt, then the Tanganyika Rifles' mutiny was the first thread that caused it to come loose. From that moment on, it has been a long, drawn-out process of unravelling.

I don't know how or when it will stop, which is why I am now putting all my faith in you. Hand on heart, it frightens me to think you are my only hope—my effete socialist boy. But there you have it. I've never been one to mince my words, dear, and you know that, so I'm certainly not going to start self-censoring now.

I don't want you to think that Kambona was two-faced. That is not at all what I meant, darling. Far be it from me to cast aspersions. It's just that, to this day, no one fully understands how he managed to assuage the mutineers while preserving his role in the cabinet. After all, how does one reason with a group of men who name themselves after a lethal weapon? What can you say to someone who has lived his entire life as a third-class citizen in his own homeland? For the Tanganyika Rifles' aspiration, at its core, was about the expulsion of foreigners—a sentiment with which you will no doubt sympathize. But let us leave your judgements out of this, Zain.

On the surface, the mutineers wanted more money and greater authority. Beyond these demands, they felt the nation had been ill-served by its European overlords. Objectively, they were correct. Let us not be euphemistic: Tanzania was more than just ill-served by its colonizers. The nation of Tanzania, Tanganyika, German East Africa—all names for the same beautiful realm—was raped, looted, and lorded over by its various colonial masters.

Kambona, the intelligent and astute operator, must have played the role of éminence grise to Nyerere. I can just imagine it: the handsome Oscar, with his perfectly parted hair, convincing the idealistic Julius that their beloved Tanzania was fundamentally ungovernable so long as the whites— *mzungus*—and their underlings—the Mwarabus and Muindis—held the true reins of power: money. It was a hierarchy that placed Tanzanians at the bottom.

When the dust finally settled after January 1964, Kambona would have returned to the reassembled cabinet and told his fellow ministers that Tanzania was theirs for the taking, if only they would rise to the occasion. How else to explain the drastic policy— almost a coup, really—that the TANU government took in April of 1971?

I know you are on the edge of your seat, but you must wait patiently for the full explanation. I also know you well enough to assume that you will side with Kambona. You were always so supportive of the underdogs. But Oscar Kambona was no underdog. He was a serious power player.

By failing to quell the discontent which first manifested in January 1964, the government allowed the sleeping giant of Tanzanians' resentment of their foreign occupiers to fester until it reached its crescendo seven years later.

Chapter 3

On that blazing-hot morning in January 1964, I bravely donned my Monday best: a white silk poet blouse featuring full bishop sleeves, accompanied by a purple skirt with seashells embossed in the print. I had fashioned the skirt myself from some patterned kanga material I'd found in Kanga King on Mosque Street, one of my favorite fabric shops near the Askari monument.

I was also wearing my fabulous amethyst earrings with little white feathers hanging beneath the stones, and a thick gold rope-like necklace which had been gifted to me by my mother on my twenty-first birthday. My pretty little feet bore a pair of adorable white slingback sandals in case I needed to make a quick getaway from the soldiers. I can hear your criticism already, son. You're wondering, *Who wears white shoes in dusty Dar?*

I just *had* to look good. It bears repeating—I was quite a dish. I know I'm living in the past, but frankly it's much more charming than the place in which I find myself currently residing.

While I wanted to show the mutineers that I did not fear them, inwardly I was trembling. I could not stop thinking about the sweet little children at school, lined up so nicely in their uniforms—ties and bows and smiles all in place. In my life's unravelling quilt, I've had an existence of putting on appearances and pretending that all is well. But things weren't tickety-boo back then, and they certainly aren't now. Mind you, a good outfit goes a long way.

I drove myself the few blocks to school on the other side of Upanga, our beautiful, largely residential section of Dar es Salaam's Ilala District. Everything I loved was contained in this microcosm of heavenly Dar: our house, my family, the school, my friends, the mango tree in our front garden, row after row of bougainvillea flowers. And most of all, the sea. I could have walked to work, but Ma would not hear of it.

Ma was a principled woman and wouldn't dream of asking Ramzani, our driver, to follow me. Ramzani was an equally principled man, so follow me he did, using my father's car. Have you ever noticed how truly upstanding people are constantly struggling to prove their worthiness? Whereas people in the wrong appear firmly convinced of their goodness. Ramzani and Ma were exceptionally unselfish individuals whom I loved very much. The most significant thing I can bequeath you, son, is a legacy of love.

As I was driving, I spotted Ramzani in my rearview mirror. I would have recognized that green Peugeot anywhere. It was a left-hand drive, which he kept in lustrous condition. Too scared to hit the brakes, wave him down and implore him to return home, I continued cruising along Aly Khan Road until I reached the Aga Khan School.

I parked in front of the white school buildings—festooned in bougainvillea, as they were—just as I would on a normal working day. Very slowly, I slinked out of the motor car, and could see Ramzani lingering just behind on the main road. While no one had bothered me, the Peugeot had been intercepted. A tall, uniformed man brandishing an enormous rifle was gesturing at Ramzani as if to say, *Move along!*

I could not tell from that distance whether the man with the rifle was a soldier or just a rabble-rouser. It later came out that all sorts of malcontents and misfits had used the atmosphere of uncertainty to vent their frustrations and add to the mayhem. That is another life lesson, son: some people will take advantage of any misfortune to advance their own cause. It makes me sick.

Of course, this is not *Aesop's Fables*, darling, and I do bear some responsibility for what happened to my beautiful country, so let me not get carried away with philosophical observations. Your mother is a morally spent woman. I make no bones about it. Back in '64, I thought I could make something of my life and help others. Now all my energy is devoted to helping you, even if you don't fully understand that you need the help.

The sun was scorching hot above me, turning my beehive hairdo into its very own mini-sauna. I was standing alone in the tree-lined drive of the school, pondering my next step. Ramzani had steered the Peugeot out of my line of sight, and I hesitated to move; I did not want to attract the attention of the tall man with the rifle. Perhaps Ramzani's departure was for the best—our understanding remained unspoken and would have come undone had he pulled into the Aga Khan School.

Such are the niceties of etiquette when someone in your employ—whom you love dearly—decides to risk their life for you, of their own volition. I tried not to think about the danger he might be facing at that moment.

I had forgotten this detail until now, but I recited a prayer for dear Ramzani—a desperate motion on my part, for I have generally shied away from making specific requests of God.

Most things in my life have come to me unbidden, both the gifts and the gift horses. I remember my mother extolling the virtues of praying for others. She claimed that such prayers are always efficacious, for they are selfless, and God admires selflessness. I certainly believed my mother, even if I wasn't so sure about God.

The short walk from the driveway into the stark-white school building was the quietest and eeriest I have ever undertaken. That morning, my gaudy purple skirt—for there is no other way to describe a garment bedecked with oversized seashells—was the only gleaming flourish of color in that corner of Upanga. The flutter of my amethyst and feather earrings represented an unnecessary provocation for any armed man who might be passing.

All right son, I admit it: wearing those jewels was not the wisest sartorial decision. Don't even get me started on the slingbacks! What was I thinking? Your mother lived for fashion, but even that hobbyhorse came back to haunt me, as you will learn.

Glancing out at the road from under the safe cover of the school's overhanging roof, my sightline was filled with the green fronds of the palm trees and the khaki-colored mutineers' uniforms, canopied by the all-encompassing African blue sky. I was surprised to see the school's askari, Benjamin, standing guard as if it were a regular school day.

"*Jambo*, Kaka Benjamin. How did you get here?" I knew the buses were not running.

"*Jambo*, Memsahib. I walked."

"But, brother, you live very far, do you not?"

"Yes, Memsahib. In Chanika."

"Please call me Dada Gulnar. Chanika is very far! Do you have water? Food?"

"Do not worry about me, Memsa—I mean, Dada."

"That is good, Kaka. We must not worry about such formalities, especially at a time like this. It appears that you and I are the only ones who came to school today."

"You are right, Dada. Thank goodness the totos did not come. Their parents must have listened to their radios. I have mine here." He pointed to his portable Telefunken.

"Oh, Kaka, you carried that all the way from Chanika? Please take a seat. You do not need to stand today."

"I would, but the chairs are locked inside the office, and I do not have the key."

Benjamin was correct. I peered into the window of the secretary's office, but it was dark inside. Our only hiding place from the rebels would be in one of the classrooms, but these were also locked. The staff and children were safe in their homes, but Benjamin and I were trapped outside of the school buildings.

We said little more to each other. That brief conversation was the most we had said to each other in the five years we'd worked together. While I was fluent in Swahili, I felt self-conscious about conversing in Benjamin's mother tongue, knowing he could not speak mine. It must have been sad for him to work in an educational establishment, fully aware that his own educational status would never improve.

Before you throw my privileges in my face, son, I am fully aware of them. As you read on, I hope you will agree that I did my best for everyone I met.

I offered to drive Benjamin back to Chanika, but he would not hear of it. He also refused an invitation to stay at my house until the mutiny calmed down.

Beyond these offers, what else could I say to Benjamin, apart from, "Thank you for coming to work today," and, "We will pay you a full day's wages." I wondered why this lovely man had made the long trek by foot and couldn't credit it all to his wages. Like Shabani and Ramzani, Benjamin had risked his life for me. All three men had placed my safety above their own. I felt responsible for *their* safety. In my position, it was incumbent on me to do all I could for these men.

I was truly touched by their concern. They must have all known that I would go to work that day, and they wanted to protect me. Kaka Benjamin could see that I had placed myself in danger, and I'm sure he assumed that my decision had nothing to do with my salary. We both were present because we cared.

The classrooms were boarded shut. In Tanzania, unlike this cold United Kingdom you call home, we did not need glass windows, just shutters that could be closed airtight. Sometimes the children would place their hands through the shutters when they thought the teacher was not looking, hoping for some *jugu beesi*—peanuts and popcorn.

These tasty snacks were supplied by street vendors who would later collect payment based on the appearance of the child's hand. An astute teacher like my friend Jimmy would outsmart his students, sneaking out of the classroom while a grasping student was not looking, and striking his hand with a ruler. The naughty pupil would shriek in surprise at receiving a smack instead of a snack!

On that January day, thoughts of snacks and smacks were the farthest thing from my mind. Under that oppressive sky, the equally unforgiving sunlight was creeping through the shutters of the school's reception area, reminding me of the menace of the armed men and tanks just outside the school's perimeter. I know you Brits believe that one can never get enough sun, but a few days in Dar es Salaam will soon disabuse you of that notion, darling.

The minutes—which felt like hours—I had spent thinking about how to avoid the soldiers and tanks had filled me with an inner resolve. *This is my school*, I thought. *Those hooligans will have to go through me.*

It transpired that the mutineers were reluctant to confront a lady of refinement. It was as though my foolhardiness in leaving the safety of my home had been camouflaged by my appearance. My gaudy outfit communicated the ordinariness of the day. The mutineers read my body language as indicative of my self-assurance. Those observing me closely would have noted my interactions with Shabani, Ramzani, and Benjamin, augmenting their awe for this Muindi woman who apparently commanded the loyalty of three fellow Tanzanians.

No rebel would want the public antagonizing of a headstrong *memsahib* to be added to the mounting list of crimes committed during the mutiny. As it was, their own lofty plans were starting to unravel. For one thing, President Julius Nyerere was nowhere to be found. The Tanganyika Rifles' failure to capture the president made their actions appear increasingly symbolic. The only thing worse than a botched coup was one in which the hearts and minds of the people had been turned against your cause. The minute that happened, your mutiny became mere street theatre.

I decided to turn their failing mutiny around on them. As Benjamin whispered to me that Mwalimu Nyerere had evaded the Rifles, I decided to seize the moment and march out of there. I repeated my offer to Benjamin of a lift to his home in Chanika, or shelter in my house. When he politely declined again, I quickly emptied the contents of my purse and thrust a thick wad of shillings into his hands, then trotted off to my motor car before he could return the money.

Why was I suddenly so fearless? I realized that, while I was dressed like a fashion maven, the rebels had spotted Benjamin chatting to me. They would have assumed that a lady like me, who had demonstrated the courage to leave my home unaccompanied—and was sufficiently inspiring that her *askari* would do the same—must be a formidable person, indeed. They knew that a typical woman in my place would stay at home and send someone to check on the school. At most, she might ask to be driven there. But I could see the looks of puzzlement and admiration in the rebels' eyes as your brave mother hotfooted it out of the Aga Khan School in her slingback sandals, like butter wouldn't melt.

I have always used people's underestimation of me to my own advantage, but I fear that my well-employed wiles may be coming back to haunt me. Truth be told, the skeletons of my past are not new visitors, son. They've been my constant companions in the nearly fifty years since the mutiny of '64. If I didn't feel so saddled with the stories of my life, I would not share them with you, darling. However, I think they will do you good. Whether or not you come to my rescue, you deserve to know the truth.

Chapter 4

W here was I? I must have blanked out for a moment. For I find myself on our settee, the one on which you jumped up and down as a boy—one of your few transgressions in an otherwise exemplary childhood. But I don't recall lying down here at all. I must have fainted.

I say this not to shock you, but simply as a statement of fact. Indeed, I've woken up in all kinds of places lately—the bathtub, the kitchen floor, and even the front garden, much to my embarrassment. The neighbors must be thinking, *She's gone off her rocker since her old man popped his clogs.*

One fine evening, I had been sitting in front of the house, reading my book and admiring the rose bushes. By the by, I've spruced up the garden since your father left me with a house full of memories and a lawn carpeted in weeds. I must have dropped off to sleep in my chair, because late that night a neighbor awoke me.

"Hello? Missus Jaffar? Pssst. Hello? Missus Jaffar?"

I was startled to see a tall man I did not recognize.

"Why, yes, I'm fine, thanks. Thank you for your concern."

Without another word, I picked myself up and went inside the house. If that Damaris Justice had seen me sleeping there, she would have kept on walking without concern. Mind you, I would have been awoken by her heavy footsteps.

Okay, Zain, I'll stop being nasty. But believe me, your girlfriend's mother has no reason to be off with me. I have done nothing to deserve such treatment.

Well, all right, that's not exactly true. Let's just say I had my reasons for what I did, and you are going to discover them.

That kind man who awoke me reminded me of how our beloved Streatham used to be. Do you remember racing your toy car down the pavements of Gleneagle Road as a little lad? This neighborhood used to be so relaxed. But Streatham isn't what it was once. Namely, South Brixton. Brixton isn't what it once was. Even London isn't what it once was. But then, you would expect such a statement from a sentimental mother who is haunted by, and unable to shed, the past.

New Brixtonians think they are living at the cultural vanguard because they buy plantains from Jamaican fruit sellers. I'd like to see them negotiate the streets of Dar during a mutiny, as I did in '64. Before I get too carried away, I'm humbly reminded that things didn't end so well for me in my beloved Tanzania. I know I am a woman who once wore bird feathers in her earrings. You will rightly conclude that I don't have a leg to stand on, even in my best Roger Vivier pumps. However, unlike those fruit-buying hipsters, I embodied a true dedication to my country at the time.

Back to my present predicament. I don't want you to worry, son, for am I not unwell. At least, not in any way which can be discerned by a doctor. Draped across the settee is a purple throw, in a shade not unlike that gaudy skirt I was wearing on January 20, 1964. This throw has flowers in its design rather than the seashells which festooned my skirt, and the pattern is also a little more stylized—a sort of abstract William Morris design.

As you know, I have never tired of the bright colors I used to wear in my Tanzanian heyday. Color can do so much for people with our complexion, my love. Why do you insist on wearing black? It's not good for your visual appeal, or for your aura.

There's no avoiding what's next. I'm digging deeper and into a past that becomes murkier with increased scrutiny. While it might be better to leave well enough alone, it would be a terrible disservice to you. I must provide a full account of the days after January 20, 1964. I know I talk of Chanels and Diors, but you must know by now that people who need to display such accoutrements do so only because they feel inadequate in some aspect of their lives.

I wasn't born with a silver spoon in my mouth. Although we never wanted for anything, and my parents descended from noble provenance, my early years in Tanzania were a far cry from my heyday in the 1960s. During my childhood, we didn't have a flush toilet, an indoor waterspout, or even electricity. Your dear mother had to make do with a hole in the ground sporting two bricks on either side. Not the powder rooms to which she has become accustomed.

Water for baths had to be boiled on the stove in the *lavani*, transported to the bathroom in a cast iron pot, and mixed with cold water for all nine of us to bathe daily. When my siblings and I were still little and being cared for by our *ayas*, they would sometimes sleep in our house. I distinctly re-

member the fetid smell of burning kerosene in the lamps by which we ate
our evening meals.

Look down your nose at your glamourous mother if you must, son. But
know that she is very aware of her humble beginnings. Or perhaps you'll
look up to me, now that you've learned that I had to rough it for the first
few years of my life. I truly don't know where I went wrong as a mother.
Trying to understand you is a full-time job—one at which I've admittedly
not done very well.

There. I've said it.

I think you secretly love me, but outwardly resent me. I sometimes
ask myself how this being I birthed and nurtured, fed and clothed, loved
with every scintilla of my being, could turn around and disapprove of my
views. Is it more important for you to be right, than for you to simply love
your mum?

And now it looks like my fortunes are once again reversing. I don't
mean that I shall have to use a squat lavatory, my darling Zainy. I mean that
I feel myself being pulled back to that place, those times, when I believed
in Tanzania and wanted it to be my permanent home, until that became
untenable.

You may well ask, why now? More to the point, you will note that—in
your view—I'm using your father's death to characterize my life as one
big melodramatic tableau. You picture me as a lonely old widow painting a
pastiche in which she stars as the tragic heroine.

If that is what you think, you are wrong. You have always judged me,
even as you secretly admired me, and that is not right, son. I watched you
idolize your daddy, and I know he loved you with all his heart. Nothing
can diminish the beautiful relationship you two had. I just don't understand
why you seemed to take a tougher line with me. You make me out to be a
two-faced woman: half-angelic mother, and half-selfish shrew. Your questions and assumptions seem to accuse me of racism without even giving me
a chance to respond. I take this as an attack on my very being. I write this
to say that you are incorrect in that formulation of me.

I want to tell you more about Ramzani. To begin with, he was beauty, benevolence, and grace all rolled into one. I've never admired a man
more than I admired him. I loved your father, of course, so don't you start
judging—or continuing to judge. But it's not the same kind of love. I chose
your father. Ramzani had always been a fixture in my life. I found it so incredibly demeaning to call him the family's driver, though that was his job.
I think of him as a friend, a mentor, a confidant, a big brother, and a role
model. A father figure, really. He was more of a daddy to me than my own
bapa, who wouldn't say boo to a goose.

There was nothing I wouldn't do for Ramzani, which might explain why he risked his life by following me to school on January 20, 1964. You'll quickly throw words like *servant* and *exploitation* in my face—those perennial little hand grenades of judgement. What can I say in my defense? Am I personally responsible for the structural economic factors that kept a man like Ramzani in our employ for more than thirty years?

Remember, this was a man I looked up to as a little girl, a teenager, and a grown woman. I adored him. Was it my choice to bring him into my sphere? No. Relationships are not always so clear-cut, my dear boy. It's more complicated than what your liberal heroes—Mills, Hobbes, and Locke—had to say on the subject. We humans are not just cold, self-serving individuals.

I'm sorry for the indignation. I find it exhausting dredging up all these memories, son. Nonetheless, it is a worthwhile endeavor. I can feel one of my dizzy spells coming on, but I will plow on. I don't want you to worry about me, Zain. If you want to do something for me, trying challenging some of the assumptions in that stubborn mind of yours.

Do you want to hear something amazing? Ramzani used to tell me that he did things with me that he did not do with his own children. I don't just mean teaching me how to drive a car, or always looking out for my safety. I mean talking about stories we would read in the *Tanganyika Daily*. I mean laughing together at my younger sister Zarin's constant attempts to not stall her car. I mean the two of us sitting underneath my mother's mango tree, drinking tea, talking about our old house in Kariakoo.

And don't you dare sully this with capitalism or money, arguing that Ramzani only did those things because he was in our employ. What we both felt was real. He loved me and I loved him, and nothing can change that fact.

Why did I not I keep in touch with Ramzani? Could I not have sponsored his immigration to the United Kingdom? Those are fair questions which will surely be answered in these pages. After January 20, 1964, I was forever altered. I spent years struggling just to keep myself together. I loved Tanzania so much that, when it fell apart, I did as well.

I am being truthful, not dramatic. Beautiful Tanzania and I are one, our destinies completely entangled. Your mathematical mind will comprehend this: Tanzania is my golden mean.

Now, draw your focus back to that sultry January day in 1964. I hope you can imagine how much I must have loved Ramzani. Think of my horror when I realized that he had driven himself into a sea of rifles out of concern for *me*. What if something had happened to Ramzani?

My own safety wasn't at the forefront of my concerns that day. I would never forgive myself if anything happened to Ramzani or Shabani. When I reached home, I got an earful from my mother and sibling about how foolish I had been to drive out among the tanks in the streets. That was the only time my mother ever shouted at me.

"How could you go to school, Gully? Don't you know Shabani risked his life just to come here and warn you about the *matata*?"

"Ma, I am responsible for all my staff and school children."

I dared not mention that Kaka Benjamin had also put himself in harm's way by walking all the way from Chanika.

"Fine, fine, silly girl. God help you."

"God did help me, Ma."

"*Eh-ma! Ya khuda.* Don't be too clever, *chokri.*"

"Sorry, Ma. I'm telling the truth—I prayed."

"Okay, okay. That's my good girl."

Have you noticed that mothers always treat their offspring like children, regardless of age? I'm doing it to you right now, Zainy. You must understand that it comes with the job description. Motherhood is a lifelong role.

"Come sit down and have some tea, my love. *Bichari.*"

As soon as I sat down on the sofa, Ma came over to me and rubbed my shoulders vigorously, as if her caresses could erase the day's traumas.

I quietly recited another little prayer of gratitude that Ma had not discovered Ramzani's pursuit of me in the Peugeot. As my siblings entered the living room, they all reprimanded me for driving myself to school in such circumstances, but I shrugged off their scolding.

The two men in my household, who I loved most—just as they loved me—were Shabani and Ramzani. They had known all along that I would go to school. In fact, I think Shabani came to inform me of the mutiny because he knew I would go out regardless, and he wanted me to be prepared. Shabani and Ramzani were truly angels on earth.

You see, I was forever using whatever had been given to me in life to my advantage. And that is a grand thing to do, Zain. That is, until you go too far, and it comes back into your face like a maelstrom that has been suppressed for decades. It might be too late for me now, but I'm releasing all of this with the hope that you, too, can let go of your demons, my boy. Please. This is serious.

Chapter 5

I have already told you about Ramzani. Shabani was the other light in my life. He was younger than me, and more mischievous. But I loved him just the same. It's easy to love the mischievous ones, is it not? They seem to need our love much more than the prim and proper creatures of this earth. The naughty ones who act out must be in pain, and so my heart goes out to them.

Shabani was a member of my family. My mother treated him like a son. But I know you will want to know how he came into my life. Yes, he was our employee. There. Are you happy?

Shabani performed all the jobs in the house which Ramzani—mainly concerned with the car—did not. He helped with cleaning, food preparation—but not cooking—laundry, and assisting my mother with gardening. I recall watching Ma spending time in the garden with Shabani. It was the happiest I ever saw her.

Like Ramzani, Shabani taught me about unconditional love. My mother loved him like he was her own child. But then, that was the kind of woman she was. While I imagine that our neighbors got along well with their home workers, it was a rare few who loved these employees like their own flesh and blood.

I know your father filled your head with stories about how he used to wear kanga shirts to represent his solidarity with ordinary Tanzanians. For a period, he even refused to eat with his family, instead joining the workers for their daily meal of *ugali* and *maharagwe*. While I'm sure the Jaffars' workers were glad that your daddy ate cornmeal and beans with them, Shabani was king in my mother's house.

He used to come into our Upanga home in the mornings, switch on the wireless radio and light the stove to make a pot of coffee for himself. Sitting in our front room, sipping on our best *kahava*, Shabani would absorb the radio announcer's mellifluous Swahili bulletins, while reading the *Tangan-*

yika Standard before my father had even touched the newspaper. Do you
see why I balk at the word *servant*? Shabani was like my brother, and Ma
spoiled him more than the sons she had birthed!

As my sister Zarin and I were teachers, Ma would have us help Shabani with his homework for the Anatoglo School. The two of us would walk
in the front door, both weary after a full day of teaching. Ma would push
straight past our exhaustion.

"No, girls, don't take off your shoes yet. Sit with Shabani while he
does his lessons."

"Of course, Ma. Let me just soak my feet in the—"

"No, Gully. No, Zinny. You two stay right there. I will make you some
tea, but don't move. My Shabani is not going home until he has finished his
studies. Is that understood?"

And that would be the end of the conversation.

On Eid feast days, Ma would give Shabani the day off—fully paid—
but ask him to come and collect the food she had cooked for his family. I'm
sure you understand, Zain, that I would never hire domestic staff now. But
at that time in Tanzania, it was what the standard practice for all who could
afford it. I promise you that we tried our very best to be kind employers.

Of course, this does not justify the structural inequality which forced
people to work as servants in their own country. I could feel guilty about it,
but will this help the good people of Tanzania? I confess, I sometimes feel
helpless about the situation. But then, I am only one person. The only thing
I can do is to tell you the truth as I see it.

Very well, you will concede. Shabani was well-treated by the Kassam
family, especially compared to the way others treated their workers. But
why had this man risked his life to warn me about the mutiny on January
20, 1964? After all, he was not stopping for work. If he were my brother,
would I want him to travel all the way to Upanga by foot, just to advise me
to not go to school? It is a fair question.

I cannot fathom why Shabani was so loyal to me. Yes, I helped him
with his homework. Yes, I laughed and joked with him. Yes, I loved him
like a brother. No, I would not want my brother to risk his life just to alert
me to a dangerous situation. It's quite possible that I would not have known
about the mutiny had he not come to Upanga on January 20, 1964. We did
not have the radio on that morning, and no neighbors informed us about
the Tanganyika Rifles' actions. I am eternally grateful for Shabani's coura-
geous journey to my house that morning.

I feel undeserving of such loyalty. Make note, son. Loyalty is a noble
trait. I remember how loyal your girlfriend's father, Orlando Justice, was to
Anil. On Saturdays, I would peer out into the back garden to find the two of

them chatting, while the hedges remained untrimmed. Before I could say a word, Orlando would call out:

"This is not what it looks like, Gulnar, dear."

"Oh? What it looks like is two men standing around and talking."

Your daddy would interject, "Well, yes, but..."

"But what? I don't expect Orlando, as a guest, to pick up the garden shears. But you, Anil, are just standing there like a statue. Surely you can work while chatting to your mate."

"No, Gully, it's not Anil's fault. You see, I asked for his undivided attention."

Sometimes it's best to say nothing and allow people to dig their own holes.

"You see, I was discussing a sensitive matter with him. Man-to-man. You understand?"

"Naturally." Defeated, I marched back into the house.

Orlando Justice's loyalty to your father was unwavering. Besides, Anil was always useless when it came to housework, and I was happy that he had such a good friend in Orlando.

Now is a good time to address that smelly elephant in the room. And believe me, they really do stink!

For the record, I acknowledge that your beloved Aliseeya Justice is a good partner for you. Orlando and Damaris—yet more friends who felt like family—raised her with pure love. I've never taken issue with your relationship, per se. I'll admit, I could have handled things more graciously when two you became an item. Regardless, you and I have unresolved matters that need to be addressed. Relationships take work, and ours desperately needs some. This is coming from a place of love.

I love you unconditionally, as I did Shabani. Ma taught us to love everyone, and to treat them as equals. I am aware that this was not the case in every household. Everyone will claim that they treated their workers with respect, but that is a lie. I have never heard a fellow Tanzanian say, *We treated our domestic staff poorly*. Because one cannot admit to such a thing.

Nonetheless, it remains a fact that some, if not many, must have thought less of their fellow Tanzanians, if the chain of events starting on January 20, 1964, can teach us anything. I am giving you proof positive of the injustices of that time, my son. Anyone who claims that the Muindis throughout East Africa were a benevolent presence, will never again be able to make such a claim. Go ahead and tell your friends—I don't mind. But please, just wait until I have gone.

You can even tell them about Shabani. He had always taken to me. He knew something was off about our family. We were different, not just for the kindly way we treated our workers, but even our physical appearance. Yes, my mother was born in India. And you have heard, firsthand, all about her beloved Kutch, from her when you were little. My father was born in Zanzibar. Leave aside all the clichés about Zanzibari spices, beaches, ghosts, and its horrific legacy of slave trading. Zanzibar is important to our family for other reasons.

As you know, we have slightly different complexions than other people of Muindi origin. We're not quite as tall as mzungus, but not quite as short as Mwarabus. My six siblings and I all sport flat noses with wide nostrils. Schoolchildren used to call my brother King Tut when he was little. And don't get me started on our hair! Well-dressed women would approach me in Woolworth's in Brixton to compliment me on my coiffure, and ask how I managed to achieve such lovely curls.

When we would be out walking at the beach in Oyster Bay, strangers would approach Ma and declare, "*Jambo Memsahib. Habari gani.* Your children are really Tanzanian!"

She would always take this as a compliment and thank them.

"*Jambo. Asante sana.*"

"What a lovely family! Maridadi."

I find my thoughts becoming muddled. As you know, I was never a linear storyteller. You used to berate me.

"But Mummy, how did Daddy get the water for your car if there were crocodiles in the river?"

"Oh, Zainy, he did, somehow."

Which was just not good enough for you, my little detail-obsessed skeptic. Do you remember how you used to press me for the whole story?

"Yes, but how, Mummy? How? Please tell me."

Even as a sweet little six-year-old, you berated me. You were a precocious little fellow, always digging for the truth—a journalist in the making. Do you remember what I confessed?

"There were some locals who fetched the water for him."

And so here I am once more, confessing. That tale from our honeymoon, when complete strangers obtained water for us from a crocodile-laden river, is just another example of Tanzanian people risking their lives for us. It did not seem out of the ordinary for us to receive help in that situation, but it was a matter of life or death for them.

I'm choking up already, and we've barely scratched the surface. But we must continue this journey together. I'm glad, at least, that I have told you everything that occurred on January 20, 1964. What preceded these events, and what did they lead to? Good God. I need to take a break. I need to swallow a pill. I know you'll chide me for that, too, my darling, Mr. Homeopathic. But believe me, arnica cannot help these dizzy spells. The medication I'm taking is the only thing that cures the condition I have. At least, for the time being.

At this journey's end, you might not love me as you once did, son, but it is a risk I am willing to take. For you are already so far away, beyond my reach and protection. When you have a child, you want to give to them everything. There is nothing I want from you but to accept our shared history. Why can you not just love me as I am? I am not looking for sympathy, son. But at the end of my tale, you might be able to stop the forces that are leading me, inexorably, toward calamity.

I am aware that your tolerance of my tales—even if you are concerned for my well-being—might be wearing thin. Just remember that we are all composed of the tales we are told. If you want to know who you really are, read on. No one can observe themselves from a distance. We rely on others' accounts to understand the events that unfold in our lives.

I know that you question my politics. I have already told you how my mother and I loved Shabani and Ramzani. I know that you worshipped your beloved grandmother, as you did your daddy. Is it wrong for me to be jealous of these dearly departed souls? Mind you, there is a lot more to your granny than you know. I believe that Shabani came to our door on January 20, 1964, not for my sake, but because he loved Ma with every scintilla of his being, and would do anything to protect her family.

Chapter 6

Malaika, nakupenda, malaika.

Sometimes, taking the melody away enables you to hear it more clearly. That's how I feel since we lost your father. Like that endearing Tanzanian classic, *Malaika, nakupenda, malaika*—my angel, I love you, my angel. Have you experienced true love, my angel?

Don't talk to me about your Aliseeya Justice. I don't doubt that you really love her, and that she loves you. That is not my concern. But does she know how to take care of you the way I do? You are special, Zain. Do you understand what I'm saying?

When you were little, I used to sing you to sleep with the refrain, *"Malaika, nakupenda, malaika."*

You are still my angel. True love transcends everything. True love was your father humming to me, *"Malaika, nakupenda, malaika."*

True love was my mother rocking me to sleep with, *"Malaika, nakupenda, malaika."*

True love is you and me, Zain. That's all there is. Anything less is an unworthy substitute. I can feel you fighting this. Why? Now, your father and grandmother are gone. You, too, have left me, though I'm hanging onto you by a thread.

The silence ushered in by your daddy's absence has shown me how I really am. In the wake of his death, everything is unravelling. When grief has you in its powerful grip, you feel the urge to surrender, to drown in your feelings of misery, and never leave the bed again. Since losing your grandmother, and your father, I have been tempted to succumb.

Grief can be beautiful in its own way, like an ominous thunderstorm appearing above your head, to which you have no choice but to capitulate. *Let me get soaked to the skin*, you think. *Never mind fussing and faffing with this umbrella, which is only going to let me down in the end.*

There's something pure about missing the dead so viscerally. The pain makes you feel so alive. When I'm in the thick of such a storm—as I am now—do you know what gets me out, Zain? The thought of you, dear son. For even if we never meet again, I love you. That is enough for me. Truly.

Speaking of such love reminds me of my own beloved mother. Ma was an exceptional human being, the likes of which we will never again see in our lifetimes. She was a giant, though only five-feet tall and unassuming in appearance. Her hennaed orange hair and benevolent smile remain emblazoned on my mind.

Ma's father came from Kutch, British India's remotest outpost on the Arabian Sea. Try to imagine your grandmother at twelve years old, stepping off a trawler, setting foot on solid ground after weeks at sea. She was a mere girl, still playing with dolls, when she was married to my father. Transported from the desert village of Mundra, with her husband and father-in-law, to a colony ruled by Germans and inhabited by Tanzanians, Arabs, Brits, and a few scattered Indians trading in dry goods, as my father did.

Ma suddenly finds herself in this strange new land, having to learn Swahili words so that she can survive: *jikoni*—kitchen, *maziwa*—milk, *mayay*—egg, *asante*—thank you. A woman who was never permitted to leave her home to fetch water, is now mixing with all sorts of people who speak different languages. But she never complains.

After her arrival in German East Africa, in 1913, Ma got word that her father had passed away. Her mother had died just before her departure for Africa. She is a twelve-year-old orphan on a new continent. Her three younger sisters are now also orphans.

These sisters are sent to Bombay and raised by strangers. She will see her sisters again, but not for a half-century. What did that feel like? It brings tears to my eyes just to imagine it. And imagine it I do. For my mother said very little about her feelings. We knew the history of the events, but questions like, "How did that make you feel?" were not *au fait* in those days. In fact, I believe you made more headway in understanding your beloved grandmother than I did, my little truth digger.

Just as Ma had to learn Swahili for her sustenance, so, too, you learned rudimentary Kutchi. And more importantly, you understood that particular dialect of love which your grandmother spoke, and she told you about her father, who would gaze into the palm trees sheltering his fields. Upon spotting his four daughters atop the trunks, he would call out, "Naar, munji chaar chakliyun vetyun ain!"—*Look, my four birds are sitting up there!*

Ma had tears in her eyes whenever she recalled this memory. Those tears represent our legacy of love, son. They inhabit my eyes now, and I have no doubt they will flow in yours as you read this. A father's love for his child—what a profound thing of beauty that is. I know what your father meant to you. So stay with me.

My mother, Kulsum, at the age of twelve—still a child, really—is thrust onto the turbulent landscape of German East Africa. All we know of that time is what I have pieced together from your auntie Roshan Ara's tales. She was not yet born, but like you, she possesses a gift for seeping stories into her brain, like a sponge that craves nostalgia. Eventually, if it has not wrung out, the sponge becomes heavy and overburdened with memories, which is how I feel now.

From her stories, I gather that my parents ran a modest market stall in Kiefmangau, near Bagamoyo. What would a twelve-year-old woman from Kutch know about selling cassava and spices to Tanzanians? How brave Ma was. No wonder she was always so compassionate toward everyone.

On the eve of the first World War, a German officer came to my parents' tent—they were staying in a makeshift camp—and told them, "The British are coming. If you want to live, you must leave now."

In the dark of night, my mother collected all the gold she possessed—gifted from her father, for her marriage—wrapped it in a cloth, and placed it under her dress, securely fastening it around her waist. The three of them—Ma, her husband, and her father-in-law—set off on foot, using only their weary eyes and the moonlight to trace their steps. Following the coastline south, they walked the sixty kilometers from Bagamoyo to Dar es Salaam. At one point, while crossing a river, my father and grandfather waded in up to their knees while still dressed in their suits, and carried Ma between them, hoisting her upon their shoulders. From my honeymoon story, you know what creatures lurk in Tanzania's rivers, and how dangerous this journey would have been.

From such humble beginnings, the gold trinkets hidden under Ma's dress procured enough to create our family's prosperity: our first Kariakoo home with a storefront, a timber business, and finally, the townhouse in Upanga. So you see—you are not the only one who escaped. My mother escaped, and so did I.

I would never have left Tanzania of my own volition. But, as with my mother, when the moment came to leave, there was scarcely a second to think twice. The only view of all I had lost was retrospective.

Chapter 7

Glasgow, 2011

Zain Jaffar had read over the letters from his mother so many times that he had memorized their contents. He'd always been more comfortable with words than with people, and memorization came naturally to him.

His mother's tales of Africa, while regaling, also contained an undertone of menace. *No one writes without an agenda*, thought the journalist in Zain. Even a casual *How are you?* letter was possessed of the agenda, *Remember me!*

Zain had hidden the stack of his mother's letters in a desk drawer at work. Although the newspaper didn't grant him a private office, it was far better than Aliseeya discovering them in his dressing table. Zain was sure she would have a conniption if she found out that his mother had been writing to him so profusely.

He happened upon the first letter sitting there in the mailbox one morning, a few months after his father had passed away, and ever since then he was sure to take on the task of checking the mail as part of his daily routine. Aliseeya was oblivious. As she often left Glasgow for work, Zain was tasked with maintaining order in their household. If the couple had wanted children, Zain would have performed the role of stay-at-home parent. They had never discussed the possibility—a strange thing for two only children who had grown up longing for siblings. Luckily for Zain and Aliseeya, they had enjoyed each other's company as children, and had found each other again as adults.

Since Zain and Aliseeya had gotten together almost five years ago, he felt caught between his girlfriend and his mother. Both were powerful women who commanded him without pause. This generally made life easier for him, a person naturally hesitant to make decisions, and fearful of the unexpected. Zain felt caught in the middle of the stalemate between Aliseeya and Gulnar because he could see the argument on both sides. Aliseeya was well within her rights to be cross with Gulnar for the stunt she had pulled. On the other hand, Zain had always admired his mother, and felt unable to confront her about the situation. Gulnar never shied away from playing the maternal trump card: "I gave birth to you!"

Zain had loved his father as well—tenderly—but his mother loomed larger as a figure in his life. She was like a military commander, a person not to be trifled with. Mother and son had shared their laughs, their secrets, their stories. But above all else, Gulnar provided Zain with the one thing he craved most—structure.

He couldn't fault his mother for taking him to task for his devotion to socialist causes—an inheritance from his father. Zain had a sharp, intelligent mind, but always felt more comfortable when there was someone ahead of him in the queue. It wasn't confidence, exactly, that he was lacking. It was his need to know with certainty—in all situations—that everything would be all right. Without this knowledge, Zain felt adrift.

This was why he found Gulnar's letters so disconcerting. He was learning things he never knew—about her being out in the streets of Dar es Salaam during a mutiny, and forming unusual bonds with her workers. He always craved certainty, and her stories were destroying the lovely notions about her Tanzanian life that Zain had believed. He felt that Gulnar's persona for all these years had been incomplete, if not an outright lie. Precision reigned supreme for Zain, and the tangled webs of her stories complicated his otherwise comfortable world of black and white.

At the same time, Zain also felt unable to discount his mother's stories. Nervous about every decision, the painful step he had taken to shut her out of his life seemed to have backfired. Her stories were coming at him from every direction. Even when he was not reading her letters, he spent all his time obsessing about them. Every word she wrote possessed a ring of truth to it. Zain was indeed a hoarder of stories, and Gulnar was using the one currency he valued most to keep him hooked.

How convenient, at a time when I want to have nothing to do with her.

He knew that the easy, breezy Dar es Salaam life described by Gulnar must have been true. He had read about all kinds of exploitation on that continent. Zain also felt that his father had been complicit in keeping this valued information from him. *I must deal with this mess on my own.*

Zain was in two minds: he wanted his mother to write more, and to stop writing altogether.

It is said that a mother will indulge her child with whatever she felt most deprived of during her own childhood. For Gulnar Jaffar, that indulgence was the telling of stories.

Zain had always been a persistent little boy, plying his parents for stories of Tanzania. After dinner, it was their ritual to sit on either side of him on the sofa, ask him what he had done at school that day, and review his homework. Once the academic discourse was completed, Zain would launch into his many questions, such as, "What was Africa like?" "How did they stop the lions from coming to your house?" "Do you miss it?" Often, his father, Anil, would stand up, caress his son's shoulder, and pronounce, "Exploitation, son."

Gulnar would stay seated next to him and answer his questions as best she could. At times, when her responses were found to be lacking, Anil would open the door, pop his head into the room, and supplement or correct her statements. For example, when Zain asked his mother how they kept all the wild animals away from the cities, and she shrugged, her husband would come in and add his two pence worth, suggesting he had been listening all along.

From a young age, Zain was most curious about how his parents could hail from this beautiful continent called Africa, that he had seen on the television: a land covered in zebras, elephants, antelopes, and rhinos. He consistently had trouble squaring those televisual images with the ones provided by his parents, which were far more ordinary: houses, schools, friends, and the beach. He was struck by a photograph of his mother dressed in a puffy blue blouse and a bright orange skirt, an enormous beehive topping her lovely head. Zain found the image captivating. She was posing next her family's radio, an enormous appliance which was larger even than the Jaffars' television set.

As Zain passed from boyhood into adolescence, the discourse veered more toward humor, with Anil often away at some socialist meeting in Central London. Zain and Gulnar would spend hours chatting on the settee. Their continual joke was about his mother swinging in a tree like a baboon.

"But Mummy, how did you listen to the radio, living in the jungle, as you were?"

"No, son, you've got it wrong. We didn't listen to the radio. We just sat high up in the trees all day long and made noises like, *hee-hee-hoo-hoo.*"

And the two would holler in laughter.

These days, laughter was a rare thing for Zain. Isolated from his home and everyone he had grown up with, except Aliseeya, he found himself alone with his thoughts. On the evenings when she was away for work, he would embark on long, solitary walks in Glasgow's West End. Highly analytical by nature, he knew that his loneliness was largely of his own making. The gauntlet had been thrown down, and he had chosen his side. It had been a source of turmoil for Zain. On the one hand, he abhorred having to make decisions. On the other, he loved precision and always knowing where he stood.

Zain saw the world in black and white terms, and could only sleep at night if he was certain that he had done the right thing. The conflict between Aliseeya and Gulnar had forced Zain to act on his instincts, and this was not something he could convey to his mother, that teller of tales and lover of words. Gulnar required and delivered an explanation for everything. It didn't matter whether she had backed him into this corner, or whether he had backed himself into it—he was in it.

Sensing his discomfort, Gulnar was trying to coax him out with her letters. For a naturally defensive person like Zain—who second-guessed every move—this caused him to grab hold of the corner's walls and dig in with more vigor. He would not be coaxed out of his comfort zone.

Chapter 8

London, 2011

My darling Zain,

I often think back to the times when we would watch Audrey Hepburn films. It was just the two of us having a good laugh and a chat! Your beloved daddy and his socialism were off at some meeting or lecture in Bloomsbury. How you and I bonded over those old films! You even made the connection between my 1960s look, and Audrey's. We both admired that bouffant hairdo. Who cares if I've kept the same do for thirty-plus years? Some things never go out of style. And if they do, then so be it. I don't mind being remembered as a fashion victim.

Do you recall *How to Steal a Million*? That tall, dreamy Peter O'Toole reminded me of your father without the big specs that used to frame his craggy, handsome face. Speaking of fathers, can you recall Hepburn's papa in the film, a toffee-nosed character named Charles Bonnet? At one point, when his forged art collection is at risk of being revealed, he decries, "We live in a crass, commercial world, with no faith or trust."

And what did Audrey do? She stood by her dear papa, even though she knew he was guilty of imitating Van Gogh paintings and passing them off as authentic specimens. Your beloved Audrey—acting as Nicole Bonnet—did not judge. Or perhaps she did, but she was able to suspend her judgement out of filial love. Well, Zainy, that is what I'm asking you to do.

I need you, son. For I fear they will come for me any day now. Though you may not have forgiven my supposed transgressions, I know you to be an exceptionally kind human being who would help anyone in need of assistance.

I really do need you, darling. I've got a double hurdle to cross. First, I must convince you that I'm not a bigot. Then, perhaps, you'll be willing to persuade them that I'm not mad. I can assure you I am neither. I was merely a party girl.

I was *the* party girl of Dar es Salaam. And Dar in those days was the place to be, darling, and our life there was quite the thing. My life consisted of parties, seaside picnics, and travels across Africa and Europe, all whilst wearing the latest fashions, some of which I sewed myself from curtain material. My clothes looked the part, even if we didn't have the fanciest boutiques in Dar.

I'm letting everything out now, son. For I've realized that the only way you'll trust me is if you feel I'm being entirely honest. Your insistence on reason makes you eminently reasonable. You'll just have to listen to me waxing lyrical about the glamourous side of my former life, and trust that the political stories which follow are also entirely true.

Our existence in Dar es Salaam in the '50s and '60s was an in-between life which would not have been possible in my mother's India, my father's Zanzibar, or in your beloved Scotland. Those were the Camelot years of my life. That they immediately followed Jackie O's period of residence in the White House, and that your father's family saw me as a glamour-puss— one of them telling me at my engagement that my tastes were too extravagant for socialist Anil—is neither here nor there. One should never have to apologize for looking good.

One Friday night, I went to the local mosque, dressed in something subdued—a simple A-line gray frock coupled with a white scarf. And then, at the behest of my girlfriends, I ran home and changed into a flashy yellow number for which I was particularly known. Everyone loved that dress, emblazoned as it was with patterns of yellow stars and white starfish. We hung out on the beach all night, joking and laughing, feasting on *jugu beesi* and *macay* on the cob, watching the powerful ocean waves, and singing old Bollywood songs. Little did we know that these good times were coming to an end, and that our days as ersatz imperial overlords—*I own it*, as you young people say—were numbered.

What had we done to bring about our own demise? When you have nowhere else to call home, you put everything into the place where you are. And while we did invest all that we owned into Tanzania, we didn't belong there. Or at least, we didn't deserve to without a more egalitarian economic system. Even I admit that. I can understand how ridiculous, how carefree, how entitled we must have appeared to ordinary Tanzanians. If you live in someone's country, build your home on their land, eat the fruits of their trees, and patronize them by employing them to clean your house, sooner or later you should expect a revolt. It will not end well. It may take decades or more, but mark my words, it will happen.

That Friday night on the beach was like any other in our beautiful Dar. The belle époque of my famous yellow dress. The decadence of our generation knew no end.

One day, while at work, I thought of a hair ribbon I wanted to wear, and sent word for Shabani to fetch it for me. Can you imagine that level of indulgence? All the while, we told ourselves that we were providing employment for Tanzanians. We were kidding ourselves.

Perhaps I am becoming nostalgic in my dotage. My mind is constantly transporting me back to Dar es Salaam. And why not? Those were my halcyon days. Yes, Zain, your mother was a party girl. I can imagine your disapproval as you glare at these words, my dear socialist son. But I'm soldiering on. I mean, did Che Guevara never have at least a little bit of fun on that motorcycle of his? He was no monk, believe me. Compared to him, I was Catherine of Siena!

My brain is racing every which way, backward and forward, and it frightens me. As long as I'm looking back, I feel golden. Those years before the Tanganyika Rifles' coup were the sunniest of my life. Everything after that has been a long slow decline leading to today. I am a suburban woman living alone with her thoughts, practically a victim of her own mind, with no one in her life but a disapproving son and a dead husband.

I knew that my charmed life would not last forever. Not even I was naive enough to believe that life would go on as it had. Not in my beloved Tanzania, or in neighboring Kenya or Uganda—our sister states in colonial hedonism. All it takes is one event— such as that blasted mutiny in 1964— to wake you up out of your dreamlike state.

By 1971, your father and I decided to leave Tanzania. We thought England would be a better place to live, but it wasn't. London in the 1970s was a nightmare: industrial strikes, rubbish on every corner, and power outages. Have you ever worked by candlelight in your office? I have. Going from our seaside life in Dar es Salaam, to a cramped bedsit in Earls Court made us feel like we had migrated *to* the Third World, not from it.

Are you upset that I am belittling your beloved Labour prime ministers of the 1970s, my boy? Well, the United Kingdom lived in misery under those two feckless fellows, Wilson and Callaghan. They didn't have the bottle that Mrs. Thatcher possessed. Yes, I'll admit it—I have always revered powerful women. But I'm getting ahead of myself.

To add insult to injury, my English colleagues—only the men, mind you—would tease me because I hailed from the jungles of Africa. One idiot even asked me, "Did you wear clothes when you lived there?" I held my tongue.

My sister Roshan Ara had not been so circumspect when she was out shopping with a friend in 1940s London, who had asked, "What will you do with all of these clothes when you return to Africa?"

Not missing a beat, Roshan Ara replied, "I shall burn them."

Her friend had meant no offense, and apologized profusely, explaining that her only points of reference were films, and these invariably portrayed Africans as wearing little more than loincloths.

When George, or Henry, or another of my colleagues took a jibe, I could have pointed out that my life in Dar was far more refined than theirs in this sad little country, with its gray skies and box houses.

You've always thought me a snob. I can't help it, darling. I'm at the end of my line, and I no longer care what anyone thinks of me. You already disapprove, I know.

I am fully aware of all the privileges I enjoyed, my little Lenin. You sit like a judge on my left shoulder, balanced by your daddy on the right. Will my tired mind ever be released from the burden of you two purists?

I was born in Dar, and I cannot change that. I did not complain when things went wrong, which is why my mind is now imploding. As a privileged Tanzanian woman, what more could I have done? This missive is not an excuse, but rather an explanation. Surely that is better than silence.

Chapter 9

Did you know that Guru Gobind Singh, a venerated Sikh soothsayer, was visited by French spiritualists during the Anglo-Sikh Wars? The Frenchmen grew fond of the guru, hanging on his every word and teaching. After some years, they returned to France. Shortly thereafter, revolution erupted in their country. You might say, by virtue of these men's travels, and their association with him, that Singh played a role in the French Revolution.

Don't scoff at me, son, as I know you are wont to do. Every person we meet brings something into our lives. The egalitarian notions which are endemic to Sikhism may well have traveled from the lips of Guru Gobind Singh into the hearts of those Frenchmen, who in turn transported them home. The French masses were hankering not only for bread, but also for a new mode of human relations.

Are you sitting down, Zain? I certainly am, in the bijou little conservatory at the back of our house. It's your house, really. Or it soon will be. I have a clear view of verdant Streatham Common, which you so enjoyed as a boy. Little did I know that your love of all things green and gray would take you up to gloomy Glasgow. Why that miserable city, of all places?

I'm sorry for being so judgmental. As I write this, I recall the acrimonious words passed between us over the years. I can see your point of view—you're not entirely to blame for your callous abandonment of me.

Back to the good stuff. Sit down, Zain, and steel yourself. After that scare with the Tanganyika Rifles in January 1964, your mother inadvertently acted as a Guru Gobind Singh for the sweeping events which were to unfurl in Tanzania.

It started with the Women's Association, of which I was an active member. As a collective, we cared about the plight of our fellow countrywomen, investing in their education, teaching them handicrafts so they could earn a livelihood, and donating ritzy cast-offs from our overstuffed wardrobes.

Even though I have not mentioned the Association, you've heard the stories about my friends and our good times in Dar. You know about the coffees, the parties, and the dresses. But that wasn't enough.

Surely, we thought, a Women's Association must be tasked with more than just fashion, recipes, and charity. How about politics? Not content with ensuring that we always looked as though we had strolled out of Givenchy, some of us thought it would be a good idea to curry favor with Tanzania's powerful elite.

The Women's Association decided to organize a tea party for the first lady of Tanzania, Mrs. Maria Nyerere, the wife of our president, Mwalimu Julius Nyerere. Little did I know that one afternoon tea would forever change the trajectory of my life and my country.

Maria Nyerere, commonly known as Mama Maria, cut a stately figure. I know that adjective is normally reserved for houses, but there was something grand about the woman. Physically, she was slight, but her persona was outsized. I hesitate to even describe her. You must be amazed that your mother knew the first lady well enough to do so. Although I only met her on two occasions, those meetings were so profound that she stayed with me— haunted me, really—for the rest of my life. She is still keeping tabs on me.

Strangely, Mrs. Nyerere and I were diametrically opposed. I was the guileless merchant's daughter who had found herself atop Dar's modest but glittering social scene by virtue of her pretty face, pleasing manner, and predilection for wearing bright colors. Like me, Maria Nyerere was a teacher, but the similarity ended there. I eschewed the spotlight, but shone gloriously in it once it was thrust upon me. Maria Nyerere had clawed her way to Mwalimu Julius's side, but her public duties never sat comfortably with her.

I hope you are still sitting down, Zain. It pains me to write this. My colleagues on the Women's Association decided it would be a good idea to subtly school Mrs. Nyerere on the proper use of cutlery and crockery, at afternoon tea. Now, don't get all het up! I know you will say that it was ignorant of us to assume that the first lady did not know how to comport herself at afternoon tea.

I'm telling you flatly, it was not my idea. Sadly, this did not prevent my colleagues from selecting me as Mama Maria's etiquette teacher, purportedly because I was Dar es Salaam's favorite style maven. It cannot have been due to my profession, as many other women in the association were also teachers. In those days, women had a choice of two careers: teacher or secretary. Or you could go straight to being a wife.

I have always wondered about my selection for the role that was to change my life. For one thing, I was not able to contest the unanimous decision of the Women's Association to put me forward like a lamb to its slaughter. Ordinarily, we would vote on all decisions. Not this time. At the start of one of our meetings, our chairwoman, Jenny, announced that it had been decided that we should host a tea party for Mrs. Nyerere.

"Wouldn't it be a good idea if Gulnar Kassam—being our most erudite and articulate literature teacher—would consent to meet with Missus Nyerere in advance, and school her—subtly, mind you—on which spoon to use for the blancmange, and so on. What do you think, ladies?"

The room fell silent.

"Why me?" I protested.

"Come now, Gully. You represent the best of us."

Jenny was using flattery to disarm me. It didn't disarm me, exactly, but it did immobilize my tongue.

"But that will be so awkward. I-I—"

Raising one eyebrow and looking at me like she had just awarded me a prize, she interrupted.

"Look, Gulnar, you will have the honor of a private audience with the first lady in the statehouse."

She was glaring at me as though it would be churlish of me to refuse the opportunity of a such a rarefied meeting with her ladyship.

All the women looked at me expectantly, various sets of heavily made-up eyes imploring me to show Mama Maria how it was done. I could detect envy. Some of the women were peering at me intently through eye lashes so laden in mascara that they looked like spiders. I had no words.

Before I could protest further, Jenny continued.

"Very well, Gulnar. Thank you, dear. Shall we carry on with our agenda, ladies?"

Jenny was the churlish one, not I.

I had choked on the words I had wanted to say: *I refuse to do it.* The thought had formed, but somehow it hadn't left my throat.

What is the lesson, my boy? If you want something done, ask a guileless person, for they will not let you down. I had bottled it.

The genius of my colleagues' plan—from their perspective—was that I would not discuss it with anyone. Not even my elder sister, Roshan Ara, who worked as legal clerk to Tanzania's Minister of Finance. Being a sensible person, she would have convinced me to stop the Women's Association from carrying out such an audacious plan and prevented me from playing such a brazen role.

Can you imagine the horror spreading through the streets of Dar if it were to become known that Gulnar Kassam—the fashionably modern English literature teacher who had so bravely stood up to Kambona's armed henchmen—was schooling the first lady on table manners? The very cheek of it! I shudder as I commit these words to paper. You must burn this once you have read it, please.

I maintain that the intentions of the Women's Associations were honorable. You know Jenny and the other women on the Association: Shillo, Parin, Nurbanu, and Maleki. They always doted on you, pinching your cheeks and imploring you to speak up. How I miss that sweet little Zain! You know those aunties to be kind and caring people. At worst, one might accuse them of naiveté. Which is not a trifling matter when you're dealing with Tanzania's first lady.

You need to understand, son, with your need for certainty and clear definitions, that it was not such a straightforward undertaking. The world was different back then. People weren't so obsessed with labels. How could we be? We occupied multiple roles in the geopolitics of Tanzania. We played the part of both colonizers and colonized.

I am not claiming victimhood—that would be unattractive, darling. We were educated women doing what we thought was best for our country. And we did see Tanzania as our country, unreservedly.

I know that your daddy never told you this, but we had been British Overseas Subjects prior to 1963. Upon independence, Britain upped sticks, and Tanganyika joined with Zanzibar, forming the Union of Tanzania. During the transition from British imperial rule, we were given the option to retain our British passports, or to acquire Tanzanian ones. Your father and I had not yet met, but we both chose Tanzanian nationality. So you see, we really did love that majestic nation. I still do.

Love is never a straightforward proposition. And in our case, it went hand-in-hand with exploitation. There. I have enunciated it. Are you satisfied, my dear boy? No, I haven't been at the sherry. For, as you know, I have never touched a drop in my life. And widowhood is no time for me to become a tippler. The room is swerving about, but for other reasons. Nonetheless, I'll carry on, son. As I recount this tale, I can hear your Kensington-schooled, liberal voice scolding me: *It was exploitation, Mother, pure and simple.*

Well, yes, Zain, it was. You've got me. Mea culpa. But please, for the love of Daddy, read on.

Chapter 10

It's a perfectly pleasant day here in London's Gleneagle Road, as it was back then in Dar es Salaam's Malik Road—a clear blue sky, a sweet breeze, and a temperature which makes you feel as though the air is kissing rather than licking you.

On the appointed day in Dar, Shabani opened the front door of our Upanga townhouse, to a government employee who had been sent by Mrs. Nyerere. He was tall, suited, and bespectacled, and wore pristine white gloves.

Jenny from the Women's Association had repeatedly forewarned me of my task—to acculturate Mrs. Nyerere for teatime table etiquette, in a manner so subtle, as not to besmirch her dignity or mine. I was well-aware of the perilous path I was about to embark upon, but it was too late to back out.

Flattered and annoyed in equal measure to have been selected for this task, I stood up from the settee and squared my shoulders opposite the tall gentleman, who looked like an obsequious jobsworth. I mean, who wears white gloves in dusty Dar es Salaam? He probably needed a new pair every day.

"Good day, Miss Kassam," he said sternly, as if he knew that I was not having a good day at all.

"Good day," I replied, unsure whether to use *sir*—patronizing?—or *brother*—too familiar? And settled, instead, on *comrade*.

He must have been a socialist like you, for I detected a momentary softening of his demeanor.

"Comrade, is it? Are you TANU supporter?"

He was referring to the Tanzanian African National Union.

"I believe in its values," was my carefully worded response.

Your mum has never lied.

The softness dissipated, and he glared at me from over the edges of his enormous spectacles. Refusing to refer to me in the first person, he continued.

"Is Miss Kassam ready for her journey?"

"I am indeed."

"Very well." He bowed awkwardly and gestured to the Mercedes Benz parked on the corner of Aly Khan Road, just beyond our front garden.

I could see that he resented having to act deferential toward me — a woman about to transported to the scene of her obeisance.

The twelve minutes it took to reach the presidential residence in Oyster Bay were the longest of my life. The driver was silent, as if it were beneath him to have to address me. I do not recall his name, which is odd. I used to ask everyone I would meet—workers, shop assistants, taxi drivers—about their names and stories. His forbidding stare caused me to hold my tongue. All I remember are his froideur and his ridiculous white gloves.

Those twelve minutes were longer than the time I was stared down by Congolese police who had pulled us over in Kinshasa to solicit bribes of salt. The twelve minutes were longer than the ones on January 20, 1964, when I had waited at school with Kaka Benjamin, praying for the Rifles' gunshots to end. They were longer than the hours I wait by the telephone for your call, Zain. You have abandoned me, my days consisting of nothing but silence. Your father would be very cross. You know that, don't you, you naughty boy?

But I digress. On that day in Dar, my wait in the Mercedes was interminable. I was about to subject myself to the ultimate scrutiny.

I was dressed in a teal chiffon dress. My hair was coiffed into a sculptural up-do, and I carried a Dior handbag. It was my battle armor for the unenviable task of schooling the first lady on which dessert spoon to use at high tea, while ostensibly representing the quintessence of British refinement.

The Ikulu was an ostentatious mansion unlike any other in Dar, with the ocean as its backdrop. A military officer garbed in full uniform stood guard at the front entrance. Unlike the driver, he greeted me warmly.

"*Jambo*, Memsahib Gulnar Abdullah Kassam. *Karibu sana.*"

I was taken aback at his knowledge of my full name.

"*Jambo*, Kaka. *Asante sana.*"

Upon entering the building, attendants breezed me past two immense carved wooden doors, indicating that I should walk down a long hall running the length of the palatial residence. At every set of doors, a minion appeared out of nowhere, allowing me entry and disappearing, like a series of cuckoo clocks.

As I was ushered into the well-appointed salon, a heavy mahogany door closing quietly behind me, I felt the sensation of a lady's maid hovering just out of sight. It was a rarefied room unlike any I had seen, sporting white walls laden with the mounted heads of various big-game animals, and enormous windows looking out onto the bay. It was the coolest, freshest room I had ever entered in that tropical city. An enormous ceiling fan was swaying overhead.

Mrs. Nyerere held out her gloved hand as though she were Queen of Tanzania. Which she was, in a way. I may have been guileless, but I was not obsequious. Nonetheless, my mother raised me well, so I reached out dutifully to shake Mrs. Nyerere's hand. She pulled back as soon as I released her hand. We appeared to be affecting a show of nonchalance. But why should the first lady of Tanzania be overawed by me? I was about to find out.

Mrs. Nyerere held court and wielded her most powerful weapon—silence. I can attest to its power as a weapon, for you are using it on me now, Zain.

Mrs. Nyerere just sat there motionless like a noble statue, glaring in a manner that she must have imagined was just benevolent enough to keep me from running. Her eyes seemed to say, *I have beckoned you, and now I need do nothing more than to behold you.*

This was unfolding exactly the opposite of how I had expected it to. I had naively supposed that I would have the upper hand. I do not know how the Women's Association had put forth the request for my audience with her, but it was evident that she was not flattered by the invitation. They should have titled it a meeting about education, cookery books, or handicrafts.

This was excruciating. I could not even mention the reason for my visit. Mrs. Nyerere was just intrigued enough to keep me baited, like a mouse before a scorpion.

I finally broke the ice.

"It is an honor to meet you, Memsahib."

"Oh, no, no, no. You may call me Memsahib Maria. For we are friends now, Miss Kassam."

I was thrown by this faux intimacy. It was hardly a benevolent act of condescension to inform me that I could address her by first name, with the prefix *Memsahib*. It felt like a trap—how could I dare challenge an assertion of friendship from the first lady?

Mrs. Nyerere must have discerned my baffled expression.

"Yes, Dada Gulnar. For we are indeed friends, are we not?"

I nodded, wordlessly.

She had used the same combination of title and forename with me, slightly putting me at ease, whilst throwing me for a loop. There was just the tiniest hint of menace, barely palpable in her question.

"Oh yes, of course we are, if you please," I fumbled.

Why did I sound like such a flunkey? It had to be my guileless manner. Never be guileless, son. It always lets you down.

I had never felt so lacking in grace in my entire life. On some level, I felt that Mrs. Nyerere knew this. Perhaps she suspected the motivation behind my visit, and was making me pay for such an affront to her dignity. The invitation from our chairwoman, Jenny, would have asked Mrs. Nyerere if she wanted to meet our most outstanding teacher before her tea with the Women's Association to acquaint her ladyship with our work in education. But her ladyship was no fool. My current predicament was proof of that.

"I see you are surprised, Dada. Do not be. I have been a great admirer of yours for some years." She smiled, but it felt baleful rather than benevolent.

"Come, sit," she commanded, the way a British person might speak to their dog.

She herself was perched on a rocking chair with its back positioned to the sea. I eased onto a grand settee made of ebony and covered in colorful kanga print cushions. Effortlessly, she picked up a bell to ring for a servant.

"I'll just ring for the tea," she said, as though ringing bells for tea were the most natural thing in the world.

It was as though she was saying, *"You may be the belle of the ball, but I have all of this,"* while surveying the finery of a room worth more than the average Tanzanian would earn in a lifetime.

Which was fine if one wanted to live in a house with animal heads mounted on its walls. My feeling of being overawed was quickly turning into chagrin.

After replacing the bell on a side table, Mrs. Nyerere's hand lingered as if she was trying to communicate something to me, and I suddenly saw what she was not so subtly pointing out. The table was covered in the same fabric as my famous yellow dress, festooned with yellow stars and white starfish.

Chapter 11

The days and weeks which followed are something of a blur. I do remember that I would receive a note from The Office of the First Lady at least once a week. Apart from on two occasions—our private audience at Ikulu, and the tea party hosted by the Women's Association—I did not meet Mrs. Nyerere face-to-face again, but our correspondence continued for seven years.

I know you will not be impressed by my connection with Mrs. Nyerere. Remember, she was married to one of Africa's brightest socialists, my little Trotsky. And I could not ignore the first lady's letters, especially not when they suggested a tide that was turning against us. It was as though my every move, my every whim—from my shopping habits to my travels—led to a distinct change in Tanzanian policy—some move designed to make life a little bit harder for my privileged lot.

You may be wondering what exactly happened at those meetings, what was written in those letters, and what was going through my well-coiffed head? Did you know that Daddy's brothers used to rib him, telling him he was dating Kilimanjaro, because of the enormous bouffant that I sported? I'm sorry to go off on one about my hair, but I have a harder and harder time focusing these days.

Now, let me think. What was so compelling about my life that Mrs. Nyerere continued to write to me? The only logical reason would be owing to my position in Dar es Salaam society.

For as far as I've brought you along on the story of my journey, none of these things can be precisely enumerated. For one thing, it has been half a century since those heady days, and the mind starts to play tricks. I know you will understand this. On one level, I was disturbed by Mrs. Nyerere's belligerent insistence in getting to know me. On another level, dredging up this history makes me wonder how my mind is sifting actual events from my erratic memories. They're not one and the same thing, you understand.

But I must remain in control of the narrative, or else these thoughts will consume me altogether. Indeed, they are off to a good start. I am not lying, however, when I say that I do not remember what Mrs. Nyerere wrote in those letters. Mostly, they were three-line edicts, or requests such as:

Dada Gulnar,

Where can one buy those brown shoes which you wore last week to see Paris When It Sizzles? *The ones with the buckles. I believe they are called pilgrim pumps.*
In solidarity, Her Excellency,
Maria Nyerere.

My mind has shut out most memories of what exactly was written, and the letters were lost when your father and I escaped to England. However, I can still convey to you the sensation I felt upon reading them. The dread, the ennui, and I'm not ashamed to admit it—the fear.

You must be wondering why I'm sharing this with you. I will be direct, son.

Have you ever felt as though you are being watched? Followed? Now imagine that this surveillance is at the hands of one of the most powerful people in the country, and perhaps you can empathize with me. To be idolized by someone—cloaked in their resentment of you—is dreadful. I wouldn't wish it on anyone.

What on earth would possess the first lady of Tanzania to whip herself up into an obsession with your inconsequential mother? From what I could deduce, she must have seen me as the quintessential colonizer. Yes, she was infinitely more powerful than me, but owing to my privileged station in life, she turned me into a scapegoat—the epitome of all that Tanzania resented about her citizens of Muindi, Mwarabu, and Mzungu origin.

To Mrs. Nyerere, I must have seemed the woman who had it all. If not, why invest the state's resources in having me followed, my fashions imitated, my sense of personal security shaken? Maria Nyerere, attempting to fill a bottomless hole of internal unworthiness, had transposed her insecurities onto me. The problem was, she had the state's apparatus at her disposal, and I had very little in comparison. She was, after all, a resident of the State House, in a country in which many of its inhabitants did not sleep under a solid roof. Who was she to look down her nose at me, imagining I was snatching the pilgrim pumps out from under every woman, and the bread out of their mouths? Perhaps she felt guilty for how much more she possessed than the average Tanzanian, and I was just a convenient patsy.

So no, I am not entirely innocent, but neither was Mrs. Nyerere. Incidentally, nor are you. For an existence of comfort relies on the act of consciously forgetting those we tread upon. The only thing that saved me from madness, dear boy, was the love of your father.

Chapter 12

Glasgow, 2011

My father? Seriously, my father? How dare you bring my father into this, you vexatious woman! Please, leave Daddy out of it. Let the man rest in peace, for heaven's sake.

Deep breaths, Zain. Just take deep breaths. You're okay. Focus on the positive. After all, Aliseeya Justice is your girlfriend. You are a lucky man. I mean, what are the odds that you would end up with someone like her? A woman who is smart, talented, kind, and beautiful. She *is* the full package. You got the inside track there, only because she was your childhood friend.

I know you always loved her, Dad. Even more than you loved me. Well, maybe just in a different way. And I'm okay with that. After all, she lost her dad when she was ten.

I know I overanalyze everything, but you cannot deny that Aliseeya Justice is the daughter you never had. Spoiling her like you did, buying her a Yashica camera and encouraging her interest in photography didn't exactly thrill her parents, I can tell you. Orlando and Damaris Justice had lofty ambitions for their only daughter. Damaris was especially protective of Aliseeya after Orlando's untimely death. I remember her diatribe upon learning of Aliseeya's career choice.

"You want to be a photographer, pickney? No, no, no, no. Me don't think so!"

"But Mum."

"Don't you *Mum* me! You ah mad mi or what? Nursing—now that offers a good, steady career. My National Health Service salary provided nicely for us, let me tell you. Especially with your papa gone. It got us this lovely house in Streatham, a Vauxhall motorcar, trips to the Caribbean every year to see your Grandmoda. None of this foolishness about running around the world, taking pictures of poor people. Nobody came and took pictures of us in Jamaica, as if we were monkeys in a zoo!"

And then she kissed her teeth, in classic Damaris Justice style, which sounded like, *Sssttwww.*

But the Justices could never say anything to you because of how close our two families were. They knew that you loved Aliseeya like she was your own. You seemed almost to apologize for me, as if saying, *"Look, my Zain is a journalist—an even less respectable career than photographer."*

So yes, I am lucky to be with Aliseeya. I am fully aware of that. But also, how unfair is it that most women won't give me the time of day because I'm…a little socially awkward? Women are such complicated creatures. Aliseeya, her mother Damaris, my dotty mother, even that Mrs. Nyerere, who sounds both awe-inspiring and menacing—proud women, the lot of them. I cannot relate. Nothing in my life makes me proud except being with Aliseeya, and that's down to good fortune rather than anything I've done.

I don't know how much more of mum I can take. I'd like to give her a piece of my mind, but I shan't. I don't like speeches, or even conversations, really. As that woman says in her letters, my silence is my greatest weapon, just as it was for Maria Nyerere. I'm using it right now, Mother. What can you do about it? Nothing. So there.

The journalist in me would like to fly straight down to Dar es Salaam and find someone whom I can ask a thousand questions about the former first lady. Foremost: Was she really the ogre represented in my mother's letters, or has Gully gone doolally?

Chapter 13

No matter how hard he tried, Zain just couldn't let it go. *She's writing about the love of my father. That's rich. How would Daddy feel now if he knew you were haranguing me with this plague of letters?*

Zain hadn't exactly chosen a favorite parent, and never wanted to take sides. But in his mind, Dad was the solid one, the one he turned to for advice. Mum had been a source of fun and frivolity—full of laughter and amity, carefree and caring in her own way, but ultimately self-absorbed. Now, she wasn't even fun anymore.

He still could not bring himself to pick up the phone and ask Gulnar to stop writing to him. Nor would he dare commit any of his own thoughts to paper. Writing for work was different. In his personal life, Zain was reticent about relationships. Experience had taught him that the less he said or wrote, the harder it was for anyone to hold him accountable. To anyone examining him, like his darling Aliseeya, this might seem calculated, transactional. But for Zain, it was a survival mechanism. He sought mathematical precision in all things, making him an excellent journalist, and a less than prolific boyfriend.

His mother's letters got him wondering about what his father saw in his mother, what the initial appeal had been—apart from her looks. Zain hadn't thought Anil so superficial as to simply have fallen for Gulnar's obvious charms. It was hard for him to imagine his serious, socialist father appreciating the appeal of a fun-loving, if well-intentioned, socialite in Dar.

Zain also questioned his mother's motivations. All this business about her schooling Mrs. Nyerere in the ways of high society seemed at odds with Zain's ideas about what an African teacher should have been doing. Why not focus on literacy, instead of hobnobbing with Tanzanian elites? Surely Anil would have felt the same way. But now, Zain would never know.

If Zain was the kind of man who demonstrated as little emotion as he could possibly get away with, Aliseeya was the partner who picked up on every cue, every nuance, even the subtlest of stirrings that might be troubling him from within. Though she knew nothing of the deluge of letters from Gulnar, she picked up on her boyfriend's general sense of malaise.

Never one to mince her words, one evening, when they were out to dinner in the West End—and his guard was down due to, perhaps, one whiskey too many—she blurted out, "Zain, you have got to talk to a grief counselor."

"Oh really? What makes you such an expert?"

As soon as the words flew out of his mouth, Zain wanted to pull them back in, roll them down his tongue, and swallow them whole.

Aliseeya had lost her father at the age of ten. She and Zain had both been only children, neighbors, childhood friends, and eventually sweethearts. And they now had the distinction of membership in this odious, fatherless club.

Pride silenced Zain.

"Cat got your tongue?" Aliseeya's gaze seemed to pierce right through him.

"I'm sorry, love."

"Sorry about what?"

If he was the reluctant speaker, she was the one who tirelessly drew him out.

"I still can't imagine what it must have been like to lose your father at such a young age. I mean, I can because I was there. I knew him. I miss him, too. Uncle Orlando was so kind. And funny! He and my dad got on like a house on fire."

"Nice try, making this an ode to Papa Justice. But let's get back on track, shall we? You're not coping well."

"No, I'm not."

Zain never dared to directly contradict her. To do so would be like staring a lion in the face, calling its bluff, and goading it, *Go ahead and eat me*. He knew better.

"Why don't you go see your GP and ask for a referral? There's no shame in seeing a counselor, you know."

He noticed how she had dropped *grief* from the counselor's title. Did she think he needed a psychiatrist? But still, when face-to-face with a lion…

"I know."

"Well, that's great that you know. And you'll agree with me now, but you won't do anything about it. Am I right? I know you better than anyone else. Except maybe your mother."

"Oh God, let's not bring her into this. And yes, you are right. You do know me."

"So why won't you try and take my suggestion to heart, just this once?"

"I…I-I just can't, is all. That's why. I've got to work this out for myself."

He couldn't tell her that talking to a counselor would take him to a place from which he could never return. Oddly, it was a place toward which Gulnar seemed to be heading.

"But why? What's so scary about talking?"

Zain found that he was in the position of having to explain his mental state to Aliseeya, even though he couldn't articulate it to himself. So he defaulted to his comfortable position of martyr.

"Aliseeya, I think the idea you have of me, when I fully express my emotions, might be fine as a fantasy, but I'm not sure you will like the reality."

It was the closest he had come to admitting that he felt less than he knew he was supposed to feel, for her or anyone else.

"You make yourself sound so cold. But it's not true. I've known you since we were babies."

"I know. Which is why I don't see why you can't just accept me the way I am."

"All right then. It's no skin off my back. I'm just concerned about you. I'm away on shoots and assignments half the time. I'm just afraid that you'll spend your time moping about—"

"I don't mope."

"Wallowing, then."

"I don't wallow."

"All right then, feeling sorry for yourself."

She had him there, and they both knew it. He took another sip of whiskey.

It was precisely his mother's pity party, expressed through her flood of letters, that he couldn't stomach. How hypocritical he was. If Zain expected precision—not to mention, integrity—from others, he was hardest on himself on that score.

"Well, all right then. What harm can it do to see my GP?"

He cleverly committed only to the first part of her suggestion, not mentioning the need for a referral to a mental health practitioner. And he knew he wouldn't do even that much. No, he would tell his line manager that he was going to the doctor's surgery, but would instead sneak off to Mitchell Library and read up on everything he could find on Maria Nyerere.

Chapter 14

London, 2011

Darling Zain,

I will come to the bit about your Daddy. But first, I must carefully retrace my steps for you after those heady, frightening days of early 1964.

I had the sense that I was captive. Not literally. Though, you youngsters these days use *that* word far too liberally, if you ask me. And no, while you didn't ask your pedantic mother, my dear, she holds the pen. And the pearls, incidentally. But then, you've always known that I wear my jewelry to sleep. It's a part of me. And besides, I want to look my most plummy, should I ever be found deceased in my bed.

Maria Nyerere was an astute woman. Forget Denis Thatcher or Hillary Clinton. Maria was the ultimate Machiavellian power behind the throne. Julius was all benevolence. Maria's subtlety was her true gift. The most potent power is that which cannot be detected. Once it has been articulated, its currency has diminished.

That was Hillary's big mistake, by the way. Positioning Bill's presidency as a two-for-one deal was ill-judged. Voters don't like to think about the machinations behind the scenes. They know it happens, but as with sausage making, most would rather not see it.

Her Excellency Maria Nyerere was not only intelligent, but also unassuming, making her all the more powerful. She matched my guilelessness with a kind of maternal benevolence, as though she were the Blessed Mother of Tanzania. Candidly, she was the sort of white-gloved matriarch one doesn't cross. I believe she wouldn't hesitate to mete out clips round the ear for her disobedient children. Just the same, she wouldn't dream of personally admonishing them—always get someone else to do your dirty work.

Maria had me right where she wanted me. I felt certain that my every move was being watched, and yet I could tell no one. First, there were the odd circumstances under which I was summoned to her, about which I could never speak. My siblings did try to get it out of me after my visit to Ikulu, but I kept *shtum*:

"Gul, Gul. What was it like?" asked my eldest sister, Roshan Ara, at dinner on the evening that I returned from the State House.

"It was lovely," I replied curtly.

All were assembled at the table: Roshan Ara; my parents; my brother Hyder Ali; his wife, Shaireen; my sister Khatoun; and my youngest sister, Zarin. My brother Qasim Ali and my sister Zaynab were living in their own homes with their spouses, sparing me more questions. The last thing I wanted was the entire family's examination of how I had handled myself in the presence of Her Greatness.

"Bas? That's all?" asked Roshan Ara.

After my mother, she was second-in-command in our family of matriarchs.

"What was Mrs. Nyerere wearing?" said Khatoun.

"What did the State House look like inside?" asked Zarin.

Unsurprising questions in a family in which appearance was so heavily emphasized.

"She was wearing a simple cream-colored frock fashioned from expensive crinoline material, white gloves, and shoes that one certainly cannot buy in this country. And she was dripping in diamonds and pearls, of course."

"That's lovely, Gully," said Zarin, herself a fashionista. "Was she nice to talk to?"

This was the trickiest bit. How to describe this powerful woman who had been strong-armed into meeting me so that I could school her on teatime etiquette? I certainly could not reveal the true purpose of my visit, or the fact that I had failed at my mission.

"She was somewhat guarded," I replied, modeling the very behavior I was describing.

"Oh yes, that makes sense. Alnoor says she is very quiet."

Roshan Ara was talking of her boss, the Minister of Finance.

"Why would she say much? In her position, she doesn't need to. I imagine that she rings a bell for her servants."

Khatoun's insights were uncanny, but I neither confirmed nor denied them. I could see she was itching to know more about the diamonds and pearls, and would ask me about them later.

My mother, sensing my discomfort, interjected.

"Okay, bas, beta. Now eat your ugali."

Ma was not one for political talk, and appeared visibly uncomfortable with our chat, perhaps because we were within earshot of Shabani. Did she sense the changes that were coming to my life? As with all mothers, feeding her child was the answer for everything.

"Some more meat, beta?" she asked.

Before I could reply, she spooned it onto my plate.

"The girl doesn't eat," my father said, using one of a handful of stock phrases he kept for each of his seven children, referring to all of us in the third person.

I cannot recall him ever saying my name.

I was about to become sick of my name, though. Mrs. Nyerere always referred to me as Miss Kassam, or Dada Gulnar. After my wedding, she never once addressed me by my married name in her letters.

The conversation at the dinner table quickly moved on to Hyder Ali's job at the bank, and his funny stories about hapless customers walking into the branch with ridiculous questions. Everyone laughed at Hyder Ali's jokes, but I was in a serious mood, unable to erase the mental image of Mrs. Nyerere gesturing toward the yellow-covered coffee table with her elegantly gloved hand. I wanted to tell my family about the yellow tablecloth which matched my famous yellow dress, but could not. Trapped between wishing to make fun of the first lady's ridiculousness—why did she obsess over little old me?—and the hint of menace, I sat in silence.

As the years passed, Mrs. Nyerere maintained the upper hand. She knew that if I ever shared the contents of her letters, no one would believe me. Or they would tell me that I should be flattered. But Zain, the attention of the powerful is never flattering. It's a constant source of peril. I feared trouble if I made the letters public.

While Tanzania wasn't as corrupt as those countries where policemen would stop cars and ask for bribes of salt, this formidable woman had the police apparatus at her beck and call. I had no doubt that Mrs. Nyerere could dispatch someone to stop me running my tongue. We both knew it, and she was beyond reproof. Her only offense was playing the hand she had been dealt, and playing to win.

One thing was certain: I wanted nothing more to do with the Women's Association. Shortly after my meeting with Mrs. Nyerere at the Ikulu, and the Association's subsequent tea party, I started plotting my escape.

Chapter 15

"How the devil have you been, Gul?" asked my best friend, Maleki, at our usual Saturday coffee spot near Oyster Bay.

She was the daughter of a count, and my most trusted confidant.

"Oh, I've been all right. Thanks," I replied listlessly.

I had skipped our coffee dates for the previous few weeks and could see the concern in her eyes. Maleki was a caring friend who could practically read my mind. So many could: I was a guileless creature.

"Really, Gully? You don't look so top notch."

"Thanks."

"I didn't mean it like that. It's just that I've never seen you wear black in the middle of summer."

Dar was in the full throttle of its February heat.

"That's all right, Maleki. I have a lot on my mind. I've been thinking that I should leave Tanzania."

"Leave Tanzania? Good golly! Why in heaven's name would you ever do that, dear? You're the Queen of Dar. The toast of the town. You won't be able to recreate what you've got here, anywhere else."

"That's just it, Maleki. I'm tired of this scene. I need a change. Do you know how exhausting it is being me?"

"Whatever do you mean?"

"You proclaim me the Queen of Dar, which is sweet of you. But I'm tired of being queen if it means that my every move is scrutinized—what I wear, what I say, which parties I attend."

"You certainly make it look like fun."

"It's not fun. And my job bleeds into my social life, especially since the attempted coup. Strangers approach me, applauding my bravery: 'Are you Miss Kassam, the head teacher? We heard about how you stood up to the Rifles.'"

"What's wrong with that?"

"Nothing is wrong with it. I'm just tired of the attention."

"This doesn't sound like the Gulnar I know."

"Doesn't it? Well, Maleki, think of how many of my pupils' families invite me to dinner. Will the rest of my evenings be spent making small talk with parents?"

"Ah yes. I see it quite clearly now. What *you* need is a man."

I failed to see the connection.

"Oh no, not that again."

We had been down this road before. A single woman over thirty finds that her romantic life is an open topic, free for all to discuss.

"Why not, Gully?"

"Marriage is not for everyone."

"Are you sure about that? What is the use of all your beauty, your glamour, your style, if you are not going to use it to advance your life?"

Maleki the utilitarian, I thought.

"Maybe I'm happy to do all of this—designing and making my own dresses, modeling in fashion shows, and so on—just for myself. It fulfills me."

"Nonsense, dear. Utter hogwash. Just tell me, what woman can be happy without a man?"

"My sister Roshan Ara, for one."

"But is she truly happy? She is certainly successful, with an important job and an impressive car. But who does she talk to at night, away from the corridors of power?"

"She talks to us, her family."

"Yes, yes, you Kassams are close. I know that. But don't you want children?"

"Ha! I am responsible for two hundred children at the school, Maleki. Isn't that enough?"

"But they are not your own."

"Is anyone really our own?" I was having an existential crisis.

"Oho! What is all this philosophical gibberish? I don't know what has gotten into you. Ever since the Tanganyika Rifles' mutiny—"

"Bas. Enough. Let's finish our coffee and then go for a walk along the beach. I feel too warm just sitting here. We can catch an ocean breeze if we promenade now."

"Very well, Gully. Just know that you can talk to me about anything."

"That's just it, Maleki—I cannot."

I sipped on the last dregs of coffee in my porcelain cup.

Chapter 16

My family had *The Tanganyika Daily*—the nation's esteemed English-language broadsheet— delivered to our door, regardless of what happened—coup, corruption, or monsoon. Of course, it helped that my father's eldest brother, Gulamhusein, was a postmaster. The daily ritual was enshrined. There would be a knock at the door, and Shabani would answer.

"Jambo bwana. Karibu."

Uncle Gulamhusein would then enter.

My father would utter the only five words he could be relied on to emit on a daily basis:

"Is there post for us?"

My uncle was not offended by my father's brusqueness. He liked that he was needed by his youngest brother.

After all the three brothers had endured, their bond was solid. Their middle brother was off in the mountains of Lushoto, living with his wife and three children, but nothing could come between the Kassam brothers.

"Yes, Abdullah, there is post."

Upon hearing this news, Shabani would go and fetch cups of tea for the two gents, and my mother would pay her respects to her brother-in-law before scurrying off to the kitchen.

One afternoon, when I was home from school, and my uncle had arrived later than was customary, a headline he read out to my father from *The Tanganyika Daily* caught my attention.

"Tanzanians Encouraged to Know Their Own Country."

"What could that possibly mean, Uncle Gulamhusein?"

"Well beta, it says here that effective immediately, every Tanzanian passport holder will be allowed only one overseas trip every four years."

"But that's mad!"

"Oh, I know, my dear. My Laila is working in Calgary just now, and I expect she will want to continue traveling."

"I thought Nyerere was a man who espoused freedom," I said.

My father's eyes bulged out of his face, but he stayed silent.

"I don't think this is aimed at the likes of you and Laila, dear," Uncle Gulamhusein said in his kindest tone. "I think Kambona's men gave old Julius quite a fright, and he is trying to restrict their movements and ability to gather funds and arms from abroad."

My uncle's subtext was clear: *You can bribe your way out.*

"It will impede my plans," I said.

For perhaps the only time in his life, my father asked me a direct question.

"What plans?"

My mother, hearing my father's voice, marched into the sitting room from the kitchen, and gently said, "*Arré*, Gully? Tell us, beta."

I knew that I had to get out of Tanzania. Like my cousin Laila, I had received the offer of a job in Calgary, though I couldn't understand what such a cold place would want with Tanzanian teachers. I couldn't picture myself teaching a room full of cowboys.

Got you, Zain! I just wanted to ensure that you're paying attention.

I may have been artless, but it was not beyond me to be tactical. I used Laila's sojourn as the perfect vehicle from which to announce my own ambitions. The distance and permanence of Calgary would serve to make my actual plans pale in comparison.

"Just like Laila, I have been offered a job in Calgary."

"What, and you'll go on your own?"

This time, it was my mother's voice sounding a note of alarm. By *on your own*, she meant *without a man.*

I went in for the kill…

"No, no, don't worry, Ma. If you think Calgary is too far, I can just go to England to study. There is a one-year course in Cambridge that I've been accepted to."

My father and uncle stared at me, aghast. On this occasion, Dad's reluctance to speak served me well.

With resignation in her voice, Ma said, "Oh, very well, my strong-headed daughter. Go abroad, but please be careful."

My father remained seated in stony silence, vexed that the women of the household were making important decisions without him. Nothing could inspire him to speak.

I had made discreet inquiries about where I might go to advance my career. I was able to leave my post with the assurance that school would employ me upon my return, although not as head teacher. For me, it was a worthwhile exchange. I was going to England on a year's scholarship to study the teaching of English literature in postcolonial contexts.

News of my departure got out, and Mrs. Nyerere wrote to me, asking to be kept informed of my whereabouts, "with a view to preserving our special friendship. You understand, Dada Gulnar."

Once it became clear that she would do nothing in her power to stop me from going to England, her letters became more intrusive, perhaps because she knew I was in thrall to her.

She wrote to ask about my financial situation: *"Might the Government of Tanzania be of any assistance to you in support of your studies?"*

Given the prohibition on taking Tanzanian currency out of the country, and the pitiful value of the shilling, only those with assets overseas could even think of traveling.

In response to her unrelenting letters—*"Please do let me know if we can help to support you, Dada Gulnar, for I am worried about your ability to survive in Britain"*—I was forced to disclose that I had a bank account in the UK. I even had to reveal that it had been opened for me by my brother Qasim Ali, when he had lived there more than a decade previously, before the ban on such foreign holdings had been put into place.

Was it mere coincidence that when I completed my studies at Cambridge in 1965, and returned to Tanzania in 1966, I learned of a new law forbidding Tanzanian citizens from owning property or other assets overseas? This law was even more stringent than the previous restrictions on transporting currency, and could result in not just a fine—one could easily bribe one's way out of such a situation—but also a prison sentence.

Despite that year and its momentous events, or perhaps because of it—from seeing tanks in the streets of Upanga in January of '64, to my first sighting of snow in the Cotswolds in January of '65—I was searching for something more. And no, it wasn't your father. I didn't meet him until after my return from Cambridge. I was searching for my place in the world—anywhere with more scope than Dar es Salaam.

After living and traveling in Europe, and returning to Africa, I could dine out for months with my stories of Piccadilly Circus and the Trevi Fountain, attending concerts by The Beatles and The Rolling Stones, and tasting steak and kidney pie. I played the role of entertainer with aplomb. But who would entertain me? My appetite had been whetted, and somehow the pretty, florid streets of the Tanzanian capital no longer held the same appeal. Not to mention the shadow of the first lady which hung over me.

I occupied my time going through the motions while plotting my future course. My American pen pal, Chris, told me to come out to Pennsylvania.

Mary Elfrick, my dear friend from Cambridge, was convinced that England was my home. Indeed, it was she who gifted me with the moniker Julie.

The strongest offer came from the people in Alberta, Canada. More than a year later, they still wanted me to teach there. It turned out, the hiring office was in Calgary, but the school itself was in a place called Ponoka, home of the province's mental health hospital.

Could I have lived in Ponoka? It's not a question you're likely to ponder, is it? If I had moved there, you might not have been born.

We humans are incorrigibly hypothetical. Decades later, I still wonder what if? What if I had gone to Canada, resisting your father's increasingly strident romantic overtures. It's a stupid thing to ponder, I know. Life has turned out just fine. Until now.

You never did care for the colonies, as you call them. Let me remind you that there are inhabitants of your beloved Glasgow who see London as an imperial power ruling over them. Hyperbolic, I know, but I always did have a flair for colorful language. Colorful everything, really. But then my flamboyant dress sense also brought me unwanted attention, as you have learned.

Irreverence is another one of my traits, darling, but I'll get to the point. You are so rational, just like your daddy, and I don't want you to put this down.

I returned from Cambridge, having toured Western Europe—France, Germany, Switzerland, Italy, Belgium, Luxembourg, Austria—and felt an overwhelming weariness. Once again, I planned my escape. The minute I did, the handsome Anil Jaffar came along—a foil to my plans.

Marriage and children were never part of my dreams, Zainy. I love you, and I loved your father, but I could have easily ended up the principal of an elementary school in Ponoka, Alberta, and I would have made a success of it. I could make any place my home if I had an audience. A life lived off-stage is not for me.

Having been to such far-flung places as Alberta, and even the northern-most reaches of your adopted Scottish homeland, I know that they would be regaled by the tales of a pretty woman from Tanzania. And I am still a pretty thing, so don't you smirk, Zain. It's not becoming of a gentleman!

Chapter 17

Maleki and I would meet for coffee every Saturday morning. This may not seem decadent in the current age of lattes, cappuccinos, and mocha-whatevers. But in 1960s Dar es Salaam, it was a real marker of status that someone should drive out to Oyster Bay expressly for the purpose of drinking a warm beverage. Remember, we had people to prepare such drinks for us at home. I didn't care one jot about status, though. I was a social butterfly.

My friends and I used to go to Naz's as a group. We would park in front of the café, and the waiter would come out and take our orders, then return with a tray full of hot teacups. When I would go shopping in town, I would pop in and order a cappuccino. I felt no compunction about spending money on coffee. Sitting down and spending time with yourself is the most precious gift you can give yourself, son.

On one occasion, Maleki invited her mother to join us for ice cream. It was the countess's first time consuming this cold confection. Upon finishing the ice cream, her mum handed the cone to Maleki, saying, "Here, dear. Please return the plate to the shop."

Maleki and I laughed, and the countess was embarrassed. Ours was not a spiteful laugh. We just found it novel and amusing that she had never encountered an ice cream cone.

I learned something that day: one must be artful. People are basically fragile. The smallest trifle can hurt someone. And it was the smallest trifle that made me turn down my first suitor.

I will not deign to describe him. As this tome is dedicated to the memory of your father, I do not want to besmirch it with traces of that unnamed man. I mention it only as he was connected to my escape from Dar. When this man learned I had been awarded a scholarship in England, he sent word, asking if he could meet with me. You understand, we had no texting in those days.

Afraid of receiving a marriage proposal, I fobbed him off with the excuse that I was unwell. Shabani went to his house to convey this message, and was pleased to do so on my behalf. I don't think Shabani would have been happy about any man taking me away from the family home. Do you know what he said about your daddy? The first time Anil came 'round to my mother's house for tea after work, he was carrying a briefcase. Thinking that this suited man was a salesman, Shabani asked what Mr. Jaffar was selling.

My sister Zarin, not missing a beat, said, "He is not selling, Shabani. He is buying."

And the two tittered off, giggling.

After Shabani conveyed the message to that man about my invented illness, I did not hear from him. There was nothing he could do. If he had sent me flowers, it would have caused scandal. I was pleased that he had apparently accepted my brush-off. But he had not. While I was at the airport collecting my boarding pass for London, an airline representative handed me an envelope with my name written in this man's handwriting. Inside was a wad of shillings equivalent to the cost of my flight. I was miffed. I wanted nothing to do with him, and he had outsmarted me. I would be forever in his debt, and being at the airport, I could not return the cash.

Exporting Tanzanian currency was forbidden, so I had to hide the money on my person. Once in London, I bought a gold necklace with the money and gifted it to my mother upon my return the following year. Ma bequeathed that same necklace to me upon her death, and I am now enclosing it here. It's yours. You understand that I cannot keep it.

You might be wondering about my first impressions of London. I know how much you love it, second only to Glasgow.

I have to say, I was not overawed. I did not find London exciting or frightening. I was relieved to have gotten away from Dar, from that man, and from Mrs. Nyerere. Being in England was just like being at home.

I stayed in Kensington for a week, for an orientation on British life, a requirement of the scholarship. It wasn't necessary for me. Having grown up in British colonial Africa, we had always lived in the shadow of the motherland. Ironically, I was being schooled in the very etiquette that I had been charged to bestow upon Mrs. Nyerere!

On the first day, we had to go around the room and introduce ourselves. When my turn came, I provided my name and its abbreviation, hoping this would make it easier for others. Betty, the kind woman leading the session, immediately dove in.

"Very well, dear. Shall I call you Goalie?"

"No. My name is Gully."

"Ghoulie?"

"Gully."

"Golly?"

Being a teacher, I tried another tack.

"It's like fully, with a G."

People always struggle with that *u* sound.

Betty replied, "Ah, yes! Gooooli. Have I got it?"

"Perhaps it would best if you addressed me by my full name."

"Gol-nar?"

"That will do." I gave up.

Those first few weeks in England were thrilling. I was happy to be away from everyone and everything. I had escaped Dar, a place I loved and could now think of fondly from a distance. I missed my family, especially Ma. I would receive regular Telexes from Roshan Ara telling me that they were keeping well.

The missives from Mrs. Nyerere continued. I could not escape her orbit. She wrote, asking about the English climate, customs, and food. She wanted to know how I was getting on with my studies, and even what kinds of frocks I was wearing in that damp Cambridge air. I was forced to fill the pages with mundane details that I hadn't even told my family. To my annoyance, she persisted in referring to me in the third person:

> *How is Miss Kassam getting on in Britain? Has she had a chance to visit Stratford, Salisbury, or Stonehenge yet? What are the ladies wearing? I always imagine them in hats. Is Miss Kassam still doing her hair in the beehive style which so suits her?*

It was exhausting. The power to ask questions of another, unfettered, is a formidable one—something I believe you young people would term *micro-aggression*. Then again, you're a journalist, so what do you know about boundaries?

Chapter 18

Everyone uses what they possess in abundance as a weapon. Your father's weapon was his interminable charm. I met him exactly two years after my tea with Mrs. Nyerere.

While I don't regret telling him everything, I believe he did not fully understand how I felt. Your father was a lovely man, but he was also enmeshed in Tanzania's political scene. When we met, his political convictions and personal desires came into conflict. He chose me over his beloved Tanzania. I wonder whether he ever regretted that choice, even in some small way. It doesn't really matter, does it? Regret is a wasted emotion.

Empathy is another pointless affection, is it not? Trying to understand another from their perspective is doomed to failure. The starting vantage point is always our own. In attempting to empathize with someone, it is one's own imagination that is employed.

Your father viewed my stories—the mutiny, the tea, and my mother's arrival in German East Africa—through the lens of a self-styled revolutionary. Somehow, his own privileges were never part of his narrative. Or perhaps he felt guilty for them.

I had hoped my stories would create understanding and intimacy between me and your dad. To be in love with someone is to want to give them everything. If you do not feel this way about your beloved Aliseeya, then you are not in love with her. I hope, for her sake and yours, that you are not keeping secrets.

Had I not shared my history with Anil, I would have felt disloyal. Stories are our most valuable currency. Openness and fidelity are intertwined. My purpose in sharing everything with you is different—I'm doing this because I fear for you. You are confused, muddled, and angry.

I accept that you are outraged with me. But I want the truth to set you free. There is nothing to be ashamed of, either in our family history, or within you. Yes, you are unique and special. But do not fear yourself, son. I am always here for you, whether or not I walk this earth.

Now that Daddy is gone, recounting these tales to you affirms that they happened. Scheherazade told stories in order to preserve her life, and so am I.

What was my weapon, you ask? Authenticity. Candor as well. Your father chose me with his eyes fully open to who I was.

There came a moment when I knew how my life with Anil would be. I felt that he was both too much and not enough, and that I could love him forever. Make no mistake, son—love takes hard work. Many times, I questioned my sanity and my resolve to stay in the marriage. But I knew he was the only man for me.

My entanglement with Tanzanian politics had changed my ambitions. Whereas I previously wanted complete freedom, I now saw a more domesticated future for myself. If that was to be my fate, I wanted it to be with Anil Jaffar by my side.

One day he asked me, "What are your thoughts on the future, Gully?"

"To which future are you referring?"

"Yours."

"I plan to live."

Your mother has always been a droll woman, Zain.

"Don't be glib."

"All right. Frankly, Dar doesn't feel like home, the way it used to."

"How did your experience of living in England change you?"

"It made me realize that I could live anywhere. But it didn't create a distance between me and Dar. On the contrary, it made me miss it. Not as it is now, but as it was before."

"Before what? Independence?"

"No. Of course not. Though, let's be honest—life was pretty good until recently."

"I can't believe you are saying this!"

"I think it's more honest to acknowledge that I benefitted from colonial rule while opposing it in principle. It's not a justification. I'm simply stating that we had comfortable lives. The moral question is on top of that, not separate from it."

"How do you mean?"

For once, your clever daddy was befuddled.

"Suppose I took the opposite tack and said, 'Oh yes, things were terrible under British rule.' I would then be denying the privileges I enjoyed. My words wouldn't magically erase that privilege."

Daddy was incensed!

"Oho! What you're doing is separating yourself from ordinary Tanzanians. You're saying, 'I was fine under British rule.'"

"Yes to the latter. No to the former."

"But you are. Ordinary Tanzanians were not better off under British rule."

"I am aware of that. But I was. I cannot deny that fact. I am neither entirely to blame for Tanzanians' suffering, nor entirely absolved of it. Life is not so cut and dry, Anil."

"For me, it is," he retorted.

Well then, you are a fool, I thought.

But your father was no fool. He was an empath. Tanzania's pain was *his* pain. He identified with his family's employees so keenly that he took his meals with them, refusing to eat with his parents and siblings. I'm sure the workers appreciated this show of solidarity, but it did not eradicate the structural inequality that shaped their lives.

Remember what I said about the futility of empathy? Anil's empathizing with his workers only resulted in a symbolic gesture.

Weighing up the gifts and foibles of the man I loved, I did the same as countless women before me. I held my tongue, realizing that Anil was my best chance for happiness.

"Well then, I think I'm done for this country, Anil. I evidently cannot live here without my quotidian existence damaging Tanzania."

"So you're just going to give up?"

"On Tanzania, perhaps. On you, never."

"I am Tanzania," he proclaimed.

What could I say in response? Anil's naiveté was astounding, but it was a facet of his idealism—his most precious quality. Because of it, he stood out from all the others. I was afraid that if I tinkered with it, the whole mechanism of his beautiful mind would come crashing down, like a finely calibrated piece of machinery with a tiny flaw at its heart.

"Very well," I replied. "You are Tanzania? Let me tell you about my relationship with you."

And I proceeded to tell him everything that had happened to me since that fateful January morning, when the streets of Upanga had been festooned with tanks. The next day, he asked me to marry him.

Chapter 19

Your favorite singer, Michael Jackson, sang, "…the city winks a sleepless eye." Well, here I am in SW16, on a sultry July evening. I'm unable to sleep for the thick London air—unusual. The gaping hole in the bed next to me—still unfamiliar.

This city, despite comparisons to New York, Paris, and Tokyo, is not a round-the-clock metropolis. London is dead after eleven o'clock at night, which is just as well. But I am struggling, son. I don't know if I can go on. All I can say is that, after that fateful day in Oyster Bay—meeting Mrs. Nyerere for the first time—my life changed irreversibly. Not entirely for the worse, but it was a signal moment. One in which everything turned on its head.

I have never espoused victimhood, Zain. For the entirety of our married life, Anil and I encouraged you to understand your agency, and I admire the way you've exercised it. The true roots of your self-determination come from me, not your father, who, despite his radical politics, took little action in the face of overwhelming circumstances.

I, on the other hand, tried to countervail the train wreck that I saw headed for Tanzania. The harder I tried, the more I was stymied, like a runway model wearing impossibly high stilettos, who stumbles on the catwalk and doggedly tries to keep her balance each time she rises. Her overzealous efforts are rewarded with more falls.

It is an apt analogy for your glamour-loving mum. I had years of flouncing in Dar es Salaam's fashion shows, and during cultural events in Europe, at which I was asked to dress for Africa. I was not a modern-day Hottentot Venus. I displayed myself voluntarily, not by force. I know that fashion subjugates women because it keeps them focused on appearance. Can we overlook that for now?

In all the years I walked on runways, I never fell. In 1966, however, I did fall—for your father. I fell for the idea of living in the Western world. I fell for the notion that love would save me.

As soon as our engagement was announced, before I could even write to Mrs. Nyerere, gifts started arriving at my mother's house. Odd gifts. Once, it was a crate of bananas. Another time, it was a signed copy of Julius Nyerere's manifesto. Her people must have investigated your daddy's past. The oddest of all was a box of Government of Tanzania standard-issued stationeries. We still have the green scissors from that set, which you've seen in the drawer of the telephone table.

I felt oppressed by these gifts. And of course, for each one, I had to send an elaborate thank you note, digging deeper and deeper my hole of indebtedness to the first lady. Were there no other subjects on whom she could lavish her attentions?

I busied myself with the distractions of planning a wedding. Your father, meanwhile, was changing his views of Tanzania. Anil's relationship with his country of birth was complicated. His patriotic love transmogrified into an unequivocal worship of Julius Nyerere and his ideologies. Unimpressed by most people, he simply could not find fault with Mwalimu Julius.

But as you know, ideas about who we are, where we belong, and most importantly, who is entitled to what, are paths laden with landmines. When President Nyerere introduced mandatory national service, your daddy acquiesced, albeit with a gritting of teeth.

"I'm happy to do my part. We are all in it together," he would say. But I could see that some of the shine had come off from Saint Julius.

The mainland government's treatment of Zanzibar—that treasured island on which my father was born—disconcerted your dad. Although Anil had never been there, he always sided with the underdog. He thought it criminal that mainland Tanganyika, itself unshackled from the yoke of British rule, should now shackle its tiny island neighbor in such a yoke.

The increasingly strident tone of the nationalist fervor creeping into Tanzania was starting to put Anil on edge. We would hear shouting in the streets:

"Amandla!"—Power to the people.

"Awetu!"—Hope.

"That's all well and good."

"We are all in this equally."

"We must all be invested in our nation's future."

"Too right," Anil would say in response to the shouts.

But the rhetoric started shifting—ever so subtly—from addressing inequality to carrying out vengeance:

"Let those who have skimmed the cream off the top of the milk pay their fair share!"

Even this was acceptable to your daddy, if not to me. I acknowledge that I had skimmed more cream than he had, but I had worked for it. The gradual but unmistakable imprint of a classification system—Africans versus foreigners, the common people versus the overlords. That way, danger lay. It was classic divide and conquer. The government was not creating such divisions for the benefit of the people, but in order to amass more power.

We had many heated discussions.

Anil argued, "Such distinctions are necessary if there is to be justice for all Tanzanians—the majority of whom do not enjoy our advantages."

Revolutions have failed in countless nations, just as ours did in Tanzania. The secret? Geopolitical changes must be undertaken with sensitivity, judiciousness, and humanity. This is a lot to ask of those who have been kept down and suddenly find themselves in power, heady and hungry. If the people who climb to the top cannot contain their desire to punish the beneficiaries—real and imagined—of previous regimes, the whole enterprise comes crashing down. I am sure you can surmise the rest, my dear boy. Humans are so tragically predictable, are they not?

We packed our bags for Europe. Daddy and I left in the dead of night, informing only our mothers about our departure. We traveled to the airport with the smallest of suitcases, leaving all our worldly possessions behind in our barely lived-in Karimabad flat. We had been able to buy a ticket to London in the name of Anil Jaffar without difficulty. My ticket to London could not be issued, as we were only allowed to leave Tanzania once every four years.

I purchased a round-the-world travel voucher with no name on it, and a one-way ticket to Nairobi. The travel ban excluded East African countries. We flew to Nairobi, where I changed my voucher into a flight to London via Brussels, on Sabena Airlines. As Kenyan authorities were in no position to enforce Tanzanian travel restrictions, I was free.

The few items of clothing we took were our only physical remnants of home. Our apartment sat empty—the bed made but not slept in. I felt happy, sad, relieved, and excited. The one emotion which finally departed the minute I left Tanzanian soil was fear. I was deeply in love with your father, and love goes a long way toward canceling out the negative experiences of life.

Above all, I had managed my clandestine escape from the clutches of Maria Nyerere.

Chapter 20

Glasgow, 2011

Zain threw the stack of his mother's letters on the floor. His co-workers turned to look at him in his gray cubicle.

Smiling, he mumbled, "Oops. The bloomin' local council! They're shutting out homeless people with their new housing policy."

As he dropped down to the floor to pick them up, he saw the sparkle of the gold necklace Gulnar had sent.

Sitting at his desk, Zain noticed that he was twitching anxiously, even more than usual. *I might be odd, but at least I'm aware of it.*

He had an idea. He marched up to his manager's door, knocked, and entered.

"Sorry to interrupt, Malc, but I've just had an idea for a story. I'd like to go undercover in a homeless shelter here in the city."

"Okay? Go on."

"Well, I, uh, uh, uh…"

"Come on mate, I haven't got all day! What's the story?"

"An insider's perspective on what it's like to be homeless."

"That would be patronizing, Zain."

"No, no, hear me out. I'm not saying I could truly understand what it's like to be homeless. Well, that's the point, isn't it? We should all be able to imagine what it's like to sleep rough."

"And how exactly will your story achieve that?"

Zain was stumped.

Malcolm sighed in the manner of a father wishing his son would just be himself and not try so hard.

"All right, all right, lad. You might have something there. Just do me a favor. Get me a list of all the shelters in Glasgow. Those places can be tricky, and I want to see where exactly you're going with this."

"Oh. Okay, Malcolm, will do. I was thinking of doing a classic exposé piece."

"That's been done before. As in the *Big Issue*."

"Yes, I suppose you're right."

"What's brought this on? You seem a little stressed lately. Not just lately, but since your dad…well…"

"Yes, that's it, isn't it?"

Zain was grateful that Malcolm defaulted to the grief card.

I'll keep playing that card as long as I have to. Then again, why would he suspect anything else is wrong? It's not like receiving a barrage of letters from one's barmy mother is a common problem.

The two men looked at each other awkwardly. Zain, for all his calculated efficiency, sometimes missed basic cues.

"Well, Zain, is there anything else?"

"No, I don't think so, Malcolm. I'll get you that list of shelters, sharpish."

"Great. Thanks. Cheerio, then."

Zain, finally realizing that his boss was trying to get rid of him, backed away slowly.

At lunchtime, having secured the stack of maternal letters in his locked drawer, Zain went out, carrying the thick gold necklace in his pocket. He popped into a few pawn shops on Argyle Street and sold it to the one offering him the highest amount. While he was surprised at its value, Zain didn't really care about money. Like Aliseeya, he had always been provided for—a function of being the only child of middle-class immigrants. He just wanted that object as far away from himself as possible.

Next came the hard part. Zain wanted to donate the cash to one of the homeless shelters. Being mistrustful by nature, he was afraid to just hand it over to a worker. It might be more than they earned in a week.

I know. I'll tell Aliseeya I found the cash, and that I want to donate it to a homeless charity. She probably knows every individual running a shelter in the city.

A moment later, he realized the problem with his plan: he could not lie to her. It was bad enough that he had been keeping his mother's correspondence secret all these months. That was already eating at him. But to lie about this windfall so brazenly—to entangle her in his mother's squalid money—was beyond Zain. He didn't have the nerve. Meanwhile, the money was burning a hole in his pocket, driving him to distraction.

Back at his desk, Zain got through the afternoon by focusing on several stories under review. He found he could focus better with several tasks to hand. When assigned only one project, he would sit at his desk for hours, floundering. Switching between tasks was a more effective way for him to work. On this day, he was being particularly fidgety, catching the attention of his office mate Peter. As soon as the clock hit half past five, Peter strolled up to him.

"Come on, mate. We're goin' for a wee drink. What d'you say?"

"Well, I, uh…I should really go home and—"

"Don't be a dafty! I've been watchin' you all day, Mister Shifty. You don't wanna go home to your missus like that, do ya?"

"When you put it like that…no, I suppose I don't."

"Come on then, Zain. Get your coat."

Zain was both thankful for the friendly gesture, and flustered by the attention. For the entirety of the subway ride to the West End, his gaze was trained on the dirty carriage floor.

Zain and Peter ended up in a bar off Byres Road which formerly housed a public library, in a building topped with a grand dome. Peter ordered two cocktails—served in beer mugs—and came back to the table where Zain was waiting.

"Here y'are, mate. Get that down ya!"

"Cheers."

"Cheers, mate. Bottoms up!"

As the cold liquid hit the back of his throat, Zain felt better. *That's the ticket! This day isn't so bad after all.*

Two hours later, Aliseeya walked into their flat to find Zain lying in bed, dressed in his coat and shoes, smiling like a horse.

"Well, hello there, Mister Jaffar! Looks like someone's had a good time?"

"Aliseeya, Aliseeya, is that you? Am I awake?"

"It looks that way from where I'm standing, you old jakey!"

Zain was relieved that Aliseeya appeared amused and not annoyed. *It's not my fault that I'm naturally uptight.*

"Oh, good. I'm so glad you're here, Ali darling. I had the most wonderful dream! Are we at home?"

"Yes, Zainy. Maybe you should take off your coat and shoes? You'll be much comfier that way."

"No, no. Leave me be. Please. Please, Ali. I'm fine. I've never felt better." He was grinning from ear to ear.

"Very well. Do as you please. I'm going to cook dinner."

"Dinner? Is she coming?"

"Is who coming?"

"Oh. No one. Never mind."

"Don't be cagey with me, Z. Who is *she*?"

Blast it! I've backed myself into a corner. Quick, invent something. Doublespeed!

"My mother. I had a dream about her."

"Lord have mercy! The less Gulnar we have in our lives, the better. What's brought this on?"

"Well, I, uh…I, uh…I was walking around at lunch today, and I, uh…I found this wad of cash. When I was sleeping just now, I dreamt that mum had left it to me."

"Left it to you in her will? You dreamt that she had died? Blimey!"

"No, no, it was…it was more like a gift. I, uh…I dreamt that she sent me a gift."

"You're not making any sense."

Now's my chance to turn this hullaballoo around.

"Well, I was thinking we could give it to a homeless charity. She'd like that. I mean, *he* would. My dad, that is. Remember how much he cared about people living in poverty?"

"Sure, love. You look funny. You'd best go back to sleep. Night."

Hurrah! It worked.

Aliseeya turned off the light and left the bedroom. Zain lay awake, staring at the ceiling while wearing his silly horse's grin.

Chapter 21

London, 2011

Darling Zain,

I'm looking at a photo of us which sits in a frame on the landing at the top of the staircase. This house feels abandoned. Your father never cared for it. Or at least that's the reason I ascribe to his never doing housework. The picture was taken on our holiday in Devon, in the early 1980s. You look so happy! Why wouldn't you be? You were a mere baby. It was when you started to speak that things got complicated. But I persevered. I'm still here, am I not? Do you really think me such a bad mother?

Any road, in this picture, your sainted dad is holding you in his arms, and we're standing on a cliff overlooking the ocean at Ilfracombe. I'm looking off in the distance, wearing my fabulous pink Vera Neumann scarf over a gray tweed jacket. Although it was summer, we were still in chilly England. Daddy was wearing a beige cardigan and looked like Cary Grant vacationing in the south of France, without the sun. At least there was a big red sun on my scarf, along with beige and white flowers.

I loved Neumann's designs—they were intricate enough for those who wished to see something, and abstract enough for those, like me, who had already seen enough.

If I recall correctly, we asked some kindly old-aged pensioner to take the snap of us. And now here I am, probably older than that passing photographer. If only life could have carried on as it appeared in that picture. If only life's stories could be told in pictures, we would all have lived such grand existences. For we all curate endlessly.

But it cannot be lived that way. At least, not all the time. I know I'm being dramatic, but from where I'm sitting, the moments that were magical—like that holiday in Ilfracombe—seem few and far between.

After that fateful meeting with Mrs. Nyerere, I could never truly get away from her, even when we were separated by Saharan Africa and continental Europe. That woman got inside my head! But son, I promise you, I am not mad. What would motivate a powerful person like Mrs. Nyerere to set her minions on me, tracking me down wherever I went, and writing to ask about the most trifling details of my suburban English life? It is Maria who is mad, not I.

Is it madness to be haunted? I know that you too, are haunted. What is it that troubles you, my dear? Your compulsion for mathematical precision in everything—including emotion—worries me. I'm not casting any aspersions. I just want you to know that I am concerned. Your loving mother understands you better than anyone else. People can be so judgmental. They are so quick to ostracize if we don't conform to their expectations.

I would be casually walking in Upanga, minding my own business, and out of nowhere, some half-wit would shout out, "Oho, look! Here she comes now. Miss Glamorous."

"No, no. Miss Fashion Model."

"Oho! We must treat Dada with respect. After all, she is head teacher.

"*Bhale*: Miss Mwalimu," the other would joke.

Finally, one of them gave me a moniker that stuck.

"No, no, bhai, I've got it. Here comes Miss Tanzania."

They would applaud me as I went past. I don't have to tell you that they were men. Notice how I didn't say *gentlemen*.

Don't worry, son. I'm no shrinking flower. If any of them had wolf-whistled, I would have told them off. Not to mention what Ramzani and Shabani would have done if they had heard such disrespect. For I was only a few steps away from our front garden. But I've never needed a man to protect me. When I was at college in Nairobi, a fellow student cat-called out to me as I was walking to class.

"Hello, beautiful. Come here and talk to me."

I turned roundly on him. "Stop it at once, you shameless buffoon! Is that how you address a woman?"

He looked taken aback. Not cowering, but momentarily tongue-tied.

"Lost your bottle, have you? Besharam!"

"I'm sorry, Miss Kassam."

"You need to learn some respect for women. Don't you have a mother, or sisters?"

"Oh yes, my pretty. I have those in spades. The one thing I don't have is you."

So you see, son—labels may offend me, but they do not scare me. There is very little which frightens me. Not even being alone in this house with your father's ghost. Maria Nyerere is a different story. Even in these letters to you—in which I'm being surprisingly candid—I cannot tell you everything.

Call it what you like—imagination, hallucination, mania—but I know what I hear, what I see, what I feel. I wish I had Maria's letters to show you. Then you would know it is true.

Can you control what is in your head, my son? That's a silly question. You are so cool and rational, just like your daddy. But I am not cool, beta, and I can't control everything.

They are trying their best—by hook or by crook—to shut me up. But they will not succeed. I'm getting this all down before they take me away.

There, I've said it. I don't care what happens to me. Without your father, and only your scorn to keep me company, my life is meaningless. Taunted by my Tanzanian past, I sit here thinking of you, the only light in my life, despite your silent protestation.

Chapter 22

My darling Zain,

I've come away to the sea—to Brighton—so I can think clearly. I felt oppressed by the weight of London—all those eyes looking at me, even when I'm alone at home. I don't like being judged, and I've been around long enough to know that it happens all the time, even when it seems it is not. We've become so used to judging that it's second nature. Even things not said or done are forms of judgement. Such as your silence.

I've come to this quaint, tourist-ridden town—a microcosm of England—chippies and pubs, charity shops and discount chains dotted all around the town. You'll find lovely Victorian terraced houses mixed in, but what surrounds them is so drab that you might leave feeling worse than when you arrived. Except for seeing the greenish-blue English Channel down at the end of Queen Street. The sea always heals me.

In London, they're all out to get me—our neighbors, family members, and friends. I'm not safe anywhere, even from myself. As my comportment is slipping, I must share your father's dying wish with you while I am still able: "Make things right with Zain."

His last words were, "You have been a wonderful wife. Zain has been a wonderful son. I love you both beyond words."

When the breath finally escaped his body, I felt deep regret for the way I had handled things with you. I should have been open about everything. When our relationship went pear-shaped—with dear Aliseeya caught in the middle—that was the moment I should have let my guard down. Instead, I was silent.

I should have shared this with you, without hesitation. My darling son, I should have been generous with my words instead of withholding them. Mummy was wrong. I'm so sorry.

Now that we've got that over with, how long will you hold this antipathy for me in your heart? It is not sustainable. I've already admitted to the error of my ways. You may think me a horrible person, and not the mother you once loved fiercely. But in punishing me for my silence with your silence, do the two not cancel each other out?

My sisters never cease to remind me of my obligations as your mother. But what about your obligations to me? Do I not warrant any consideration? Have you forgotten the person who carried you inside her for nine months?

I wouldn't be so cavalier, Zain beta. One day, when you near the end of the journey, you will look back in an attempt to understand what it all meant. Without your father and I, with no wife or children, no siblings, to whom will you turn? Aliseeya's friends—the metropolitan set of Glasgow's Merchant Town—will not have the answers. You will be lost if you do not know yourself.

I know I'm partly to blame, and I'm trying to correct the record. If it is difficult for you to accept my request, then just imagine how I feel making it in the first place. What do you stand to lose? The cost of a flight to London. One weekend of your time. Your pride. But if you continue to ignore me, and they lock me up, or worse…what then?

You could reach the end of your days, ignorant of your origins, of all that your ancestors have endured. There is so much more about Mrs. Nyerere that I cannot write. Blame it on Maria—she made me this way, son. That woman tormented me until I had nothing left to give! By the time you were born, I loved you, I held you and played with you, but my heart was a desolate station.

As a young man, you asked so many questions which I left unanswered, fobbing you off on your father. I ensured that you were well-dressed, well-fed, and well-educated. The rest, I left to Daddy. That is why you so revere him. I admit it. You may think I'm playing up my victimhood, but I'm also owning it. I had agency and chose not to use it fully in your upbringing. Why? Because I was tired.

It may seem a flimsy excuse, but at the time it was all I could do to walk the streets of London, evading the Tanzanian spies lurking 'round every corner, waiting to transport me to the notorious asylums of Dodoma. I was not well, and my only remedy was silence. If I had expressed my fears, I might have been carted off to St. George's Hospital. It might still happen.

Do you understand? I held my tongue so that you would have a proper mother, not some mad Bertha Rochester figure. So I didn't answer every question. At least I was there to raise you. You would have been worse off alone with your father. No disrespect to Anil, but he couldn't organize a cup of tea. His head was in the clouds, bless him. May his soul rest in peace. I want the same for myself.

Chapter 23

Glasgow, 2010

E very Friday, Anil Jaffar would send a cheery text message to his son, Zain, to wish him a happy weekend. One Friday in May—an exceptionally fine day in ordinarily gloomy Glasgow—Zain received an unusual text:

Happy Friday ☺ Have A Nice Day ☺ Nice Weekend ☺ This message comes to you from a hospital bed where I am since last night. Thank you for your kind thoughts and prayers. No need to worry, son.

Only Daddy would be so gratuitous in his use of smiley faces.

Panicking, Zain ran out of *The Herald's* heritage building, for there was no privacy in his shared office. He rang the landline of his parents' South London house for the first time in four years. His mother answered on the first ring.

Before he had uttered a word, Gulnar declared, "I've been waiting for you. I knew you would call."

Zain wondered how she had known it was him, but he had no time for niceties.

"Which hospital is Daddy in?"

"Aren't you even going to ask your dear old mother how she is doing?"

There you go again, making it all about you. Don't you realize that I wouldn't even deign to ring you if it wasn't a matter of life and death?

"I'm sorry, Mum. I'm busy at work."

Just a few seconds into the conversation, and he was already lying. *Well done, Zain.*

"It sounds too loud for your office, darling."

"I'm a reporter, mother. I'm on the beat. This is what I do."

He was standing amidst the usual throng of shoppers in Renfield Street, but that was immaterial.

"I don't understand why you have to do such mundane, drudging work in the first—"

"Please stop. Now is not the time for one of your tirades. Will you just tell me which hospital Dad is in?"

"Saint George's. Are you coming to London?"

"Thank you. That's all I needed to know. Good day." *How have I become this person?*

"So that's it, then? This has been quite tough on me, too, you know. Don't you even want to know what happened to your poor old dad? Last night, he had a heart attack."

To engage or not to engage. That is the dilemma. Zain instinctively avoided interaction.

"Look, I hope you're okay. I'm going to try to reach Dad at Saint George's now. He's not answering his mobile." *Another layer added to my tissue of lies.*

"Okay, son."

He knew she would surmise that he would come to London.

I know I should sort out this dispute with her, but right now, Dad is my top priority.

"Bye, Mum."

"Goodbye, my darling Zainy."

After walking back up to the newspaper's first-floor offices, Zain knocked on the door of his editor's suite.

"Hullo, Malcolm. May I…may I please…have a moment of your time?"

"Come on in, Zain. It's all right. Don't be frightened."

Taking cautious steps, Zain entered his boss's room.

"What's up, then?"

"Well, uh, I…"

"It's okay, son. You can tell me."

My face is an open book, isn't it?

"It's about my dad. He's in hospital. I must go straight down to London."

"I'm sorry to hear that. Of course. You can use your annual leave. Do you need anything from me?"

Malcolm seemed slightly annoyed, but Zain couldn't quite tell. He had never been adept at reading signals.

"Cheers. I'm all right for now. I can't say when I'll be back."

"That's okay, mate. We'll cover your desk while you're gone. You just focus on helping your dad get better, d'ya hear?"

"Yep. Cheerio."

"Righty-ho."

After collecting his personal effects, Zain ran out of *The Herald*'s offices without saying goodbye to Aliseeya, Peter, or anyone else. He jogged to the subway station. As he was making his way through the Glaswegian crowds, his mind was consumed with worry about work.

Was Malcolm cheesed off with me? Will he use my absence to fire me? Calm down, Zain. You're being paranoid.

Taking the train to Hillhead, he forcibly calmed himself as he walked up the platform stairs. *Just breathe, Zain. Take a deep breath. That's it.*

Maintaining his composure, he walked at a more normal place. *I don't want people to look at me and laugh, like I'm some great big galloping horse.*

Taking measured steps down the Byres Road, in no time, Zain found himself in his Great George Street flat. He packed an overnight bag, reminded himself to breathe, and rang for a taxi to drive him to the airport. While waiting for the taxi, he wrote Aliseeya a hurried note.

Dear Ali,

I'm going to London. My dad is in hospital. Heart attack. Will keep you posted. Have mobile, will ring from Tooting (he's at St. George's). Good grief. I'm okay.

Love,

Zx

As he had just done with Gulnar, Zain was going out of his way to avoid an uncomfortable conversation with Aliseeya. He could have rung or texted her instead of writing her a note. He knew it was cowardly, but he just couldn't help himself.

Facing any emotional situation had always been his worst nightmare, so he avoided such scenarios at all costs. He feared he would break down and cry if he had talk about his feelings. He had been looking down at the floor through the entirety of his conversation with Malcolm, desperately trying to keep it together.

There was more. This was the moment he had been fearing. For quite some time, Zain had suspected that his decision to cut off contact with his mum would come back to haunt him. He could now feel the taste of regret ascending in his throat like a burning sensation.

Emotions are like monsters. Especially mine.

Knowing he was doing his best to cope did not stop the feelings of guilt from flooding in. As with all those who hold themselves to high standards, nothing was good enough for Zain. He was his own worst critic. He was also adept at equipping his critics with ammunition—his mother first in the queue. *What does she know, anyway? She has led such a sheltered life. Protected by my dad, and by her family before her marriage, a doyenne of Dar es Salaam. I need to get that woman out of my mind. Nothing good will come of these thoughts.*

Sitting in the taxi, Zain was also trying to avoid thoughts of his father. He didn't want to cry in front of the driver. *I don't want him to think me a sissy.*

He was also blocking out thoughts of Aliseeya. He knew she would be perplexed by his sudden departure. She would have offered to travel with him, if only he had waited until she finished work.

Objectively speaking, I'm a terrible son, and a terrible boyfriend. I guess that makes me a terrible person all round?

Zain felt guilty. All he wanted now was to be by his father's side. Unlike Anil, he wasn't religious. But in a moment of desperation, Zain thought his dad's heart attack might be God's punishment for abandoning his parents. He was keenly aware that his father had suffered for his mother's sins. Cutting off contact with Gulnar had surely injured his father the most—an inadvertent victim of the mother-son feud.

How could I have done this to my dad?

Anil had always been so gracious, had warmly welcomed Aliseeya into the family, and loved her like she was his own daughter, especially since she had lost her father, Orlando.

It was one thing to cut Mum out of my life. But Dad got cut in the process. Ironic, isn't it? I couldn't tolerate my mother's intolerance, and Dad got hurt.

Zain wished his mother could be more like Aliseeya's. Mrs. Justice—as he had called her all his life—was the kind of mother to put everyone else's needs before her own. If it had been Mrs. Justice he had just spoken to, she would have asked him how *he* was feeling, what his travel plans were, had he eaten, if he needed anything.

Damaris Justice descended from a line of matriarchs, and had given birth to his beloved Aliseeya, an equally formidable woman.

Chapter 24

At least I have my Aliseeya. I guess I have Missus Justice, too.

In addition to being a formidable woman, Damaris Justice was a mother, a nurse, and Zain's babysitter when he was three years old and his own mother had returned to work.

Gulnar decided that teaching in an East End school was more fulfilling than being a stay-at-home mother. The Jaffars had not needed the money, but Gulnar took the job because she could not stand to cook. Anil expected his wife to prepare the family's meals since she was at home. But if they both worked, she could feign exhaustion.

"Anil, darling, all you do is add up numbers. Whereas, I spend my days tending to the forgotten youth of Bethnal Green. Do you really expect me to clean a chicken now?"

It seemed to Zain that his mum had always possessed a talent for invoking the pity of others, and his dad had fallen for it hook, line, and sinker.

Zain might have enjoyed her colorful stories during his childhood, but now he was onto her tricks.

Once you see someone for what they really are, it's impossible to unsee it.

"Terminal one, please," he called out to the driver.

"A'right, then. Here y'are son."

After paying the cab fare, Zain ran straight to the British Midlands sales counter and bought a ticket for the next flight to Heathrow. It was leaving in an hour—just enough time for him to get through security and board the airplane.

In the midst of his frantic departure, Zain had forgotten to eat. After collapsing into his seat at the back of the aircraft, he was awakened by a flight attendant handing him a ham sandwich.

I'm too tired to ask for a vegetarian option. I can't be bothered to make a fuss.

Zain peeled the ham off and ate the plain bread, which tasted exactly like ham. He was not an observant Muslim, but at least he could maintain that he had never eaten pork. Zain's faith in God might be shaky, but now was no time to be angering Him.

Zain fell into a deep sleep, woken only by the rumbling of the aircraft as it landed.

After paying the outrageous fare from Heathrow Airport to Tooting, South London, Zain arrived at St. George's Hospital an hour before the end of visiting hours. Upon entering the cardiac ward, the nurse at reception greeted him.

"You must be Mister Jaffar's son. I hear you're a journalist. Your dad will be thrilled to bits that you've come all the way from Glasgow! He has spoken of nothing else since he was checked in."

Walking into his dad's room, Zain felt a rush to his heart—as if he had taken a stimulant—that was simultaneously elation at seeing Anil's smile of recognition, and distress at seeing him in this state. He had never seen his father in hospital before. Had never even seen him ill. He could not recall his dad having even a cold. They did not keep painkillers in the house.

"Daddy!"

"Zain, beta! Come here."

Zain embraced Anil, who was sitting upright in bed and appeared fine, apart from looking as though he had not slept.

"It's good to see you. You needn't have come all this way to see me! It was just a heart attack. Thank God your mother insisted that I come to the hospital."

"Really?"

"Yes, I'm telling you the truth. Why are you looking at me like that, son? It's nothing to worry about."

"Right. So why did you text me?"

"Don't I text you every Friday? I wasn't going to withhold this information, but I didn't mean for it to scare you."

"Should a son not be concerned about his father? Whatever you say, I had to come and see you. How are you feeling now?"

"I'm okay. Thanks, betulo. Hopefully they will release me in a day or two, and you will be able to get back to Aliseeya. How is she doing?"

Typical Dad, always asking after others rather than dwelling on his own troubles.

"She's fine. Thanks for asking."

Zain could feel his father's lie detector pricking up to attention. It was as though his big, hairy ears were hiding radars.

Anil gave him a quizzical look.

"Well, actually, I left Glasgow without speaking to her. So technically, I don't know how she is at the minute."

"Why did you do that, son?"

"Because I wanted to see you. I was worried."

"And?"

"Does there have to be an *and*, Dad?"

"No, but there is one, isn't there?"

"Well, I, uh…yes, there is. I just didn't want to restart the whole drama between Mum and Aliseeya."

"I see." Anil paused for a moment. "Son, come and sit down on the chair."

Zain did as he was told. His father continued.

"Aliseeya is more understanding than you allow. Had you spoken to her before leaving, I'm sure she would have supported your decision to come here. By not consulting her, you have excluded her. Do you see that?"

"Yes, Dad."

"So why do you always stop short of saying the things that you should? What is the matter, beta?"

"Can we please just let it go?"

"Don't be cross with me, son. I am only trying to help you."

"I know. I'm not cross."

"Are you sure?"

"Yes. Why do you ask?"

"Your mother."

"What about her?"

"She was hurt by the way you hung up the telephone on her."

Surely you can understand my reticence to speak to her.

"She was hurt? Ha! That's rich, considering the stunt she pulled four years ago."

Anil remained silent.

"So you're taking her side, then?"

"I am not taking anyone's side, betulo. I'm just relaying what Mum told me."

"Okay."

"Even though she hasn't acted in a manner that pleases you, your mother still has feelings."

Diplomatic Dad. "Oh, really? What about my feelings?"

"Nothing good has ever followed that question, son."

"How do you mean?"

"It presumes injury on the part of the one raising the question. People who see themselves as victims are dangerous, capable of lashing out at anyone because they were harmed."

"You think I'm acting like a victim?"

"Are you not?"

"No! Mum stopped speaking to me after I got together with Aliseeya. Am I not the wronged party?"

"What do you gain by seeing yourself as the wronged party?"

"Honestly, Dad! Why are you winding me up?"

"I'm doing nothing of the sort. Please keep calm, beta. I just want you to see that your life is a result of your own actions, regardless of what others do to you. Feeling wronged doesn't get you anything, does it? If your mother was wrong to exclude Aliseeya, how is your excluding Mum any better?"

"So you want me to be a saint, then. Like you?"

"There's no need to be sarcastic, son. I have never claimed to be a saint."

Zain was silently staring down.

"Zain, look at me."

He slowly peeled his gaze from the floor.

"That's better. I love you."

"I know." *I didn't come here to receive a lecture.*

"Cheer up! I know you didn't come all this way to hear a lecture from your old dad."

How do you always know what I'm thinking? "No, I didn't."

"Look, son. Your mum went home because she was tired."

Zain could also read his father's mind. Anil was really saying, *I asked her to leave so as to avoid a scene between you two.*

Be gracious, Zain. "It's good that she's gone home to rest."

"Yes, it is. This has come as quite a shock to her. She feels alone. In the past, your Aunty Damaris would have been a huge support. She works right here at Saint George's."

And whose fault is it that Missus Justice has washed her hands of Mum?

"You mustn't think ill of your mother."

I don't think ill of her. She's made her own bed, and she can lie in it.

Anil looked at him, saying nothing.

After a long minute, he asked Zain, "Have you eaten? The staff has brought me dinner, but I don't want any of it."

"I can't eat your food, Dad! You have to get well. You need it to regain your strength."

"No, I'm fine. I had an enormous lunch. And as you know, I don't normally eat lunch."

"Come on, Daddy. Do you really expect me to eat hospital food?"

"You see, my prince?" Anil was smiling.

"Do I see what?"

"However much you protest, you are still your mother's son. She wouldn't touch this hospital food with a barge pole, as she says."

Father and son shared a quiet chuckle.

That night, exhausted from his travels, Zain fell asleep in the chair next to his father's bed. It was the most comfortable place in the world for him to be.

Chapter 25

The next morning, Zain and Gulnar saw each other for the first time in four years. Sharing the small space of Anil's hospital room, mother and son were unable to break through their mutually constructed wall of rejection.

Zain berated himself for freezing out his mum. Given his coldness toward Gulnar, he questioned whether he had ever really loved her. All their years of kinship, bonhomie, and laughter had halted because of her refusal to acknowledge his relationship with Aliseeya.

Am I not doing the same thing to her that she is doing to me?

Had Aliseeya been present to capture the moment, she could have posted it on social media with the caption, *#awkward.* Though, her artistry did not stretch to uncomfortable moments in her partner's family. For her job at *The Herald,* she snapped newsworthy happenings of interest to Glaswegians, from local interest stories to international assignments. Her most frequent work trips were to Belfast, but she had been as far afield as Cairo. It was a far cry from her globetrotting days for the international newswire company in London.

Love doesn't need money, she had thought when taking the Scottish job. *It could, however, do with at least a little career satisfaction.*

On the day of Zain's sudden departure, Aliseeya had known something was off even before she read his note. She had not seen him in the office, and he had not texted her. Their usual Friday night ritual involved chatting about whether they would go out for dinner or stay in, and where they would go, or what they would cook.

Over their four years in Glasgow, the pair had built a coterie of friendships on the strength of Aliseeya's gregarious personality. Zain could be a good friend once a solid bond was formed, but he struggled to form such bonds in the first place.

Aliseeya and Zain had been friends for almost the entirety of their lives, but their romantic relationship had started at a chance reunion on his thirtieth birthday. She was in London to cover the Queen's bestowing of a knighthood to Salman Rushdie. She had missed countless birthdays of Zain's due to her travels, but she was able to attend this one.

His party consisted of a small gathering of his university friends and Streatham crew, in a Malaysian restaurant on Soho's Great Windmill Street. Zain spent most of the evening chatting with Aliseeya and ignoring his mates. Afterward, he asked himself why he hadn't noticed her in that way before. There she had been, right in front of him for literally his whole life. Perhaps he had avoided the possibility because he was cognizant of the rancor their relationship would cause between their families.

Avoid conflict at all costs. That's my motto.

However hard he tried, he could not resist Aliseeya Justice. She was tall, lean, and possessed of a confidence that disarmed the subjects whom she photographed. The simplicity of her style— close-cropped hair, plain white t-shirts, and blue jeans, accessorized only with a green-strapped solar-powered military watch—belied her intellectual complexity.

Zain found it ironic that his discerning mother had selected the Justice family as a safe haven for her overprotected son, and then flipped out when he wanted to date Aliseeya. In their childhoods, they had done everything together—birthdays, picnics, school trips, family outings. Gulnar herself had maintained a close friendship with Damaris Justice for nearly three decades. And Anil and Orlando had been like brothers until the latter's untimely death.

Gulnar had always intimated that no woman was good enough for Zain. But nothing could have prepared him for the maelstrom that was unleashed four years ago. His mother's stubborn refusal to acknowledge his relationship with Aliseeya made Zain call into question the sincerity of her friendship with Damaris Justice. If Gulnar truly regarded Damaris as a sister, would she have acted as she had?

The Jaffar–Justice division was further complicated by Anil's fatherly interest Aliseeya. He used to spend hours chatting to her about photography, travel, and world events. Gulnar seemed jealous of her husband's, and her son's, admiration for Aliseeya.

Aliseeya Justice, however, was neither a victim nor a fool. Within days of Gulnar's refusal to accept her relationship with Zain, Aliseeya was onto a contact at *The Herald,* resulting in job offers for the pair. Zain fulfilled his notice at the consumer advocacy organization where he worked as a copywriter, and Aliseeya left the newswire agency on good terms.

Ever-supportive, Anil drove the couple to Glasgow and moved them into their new flat. Living together so early on in a relationship might appear risky, but Aliseeya was confident that it would work. She had known Zain her entire life, and knew him to be a good man, however shaky.

When Aliseeya finally got hold of Zain that Saturday afternoon—a day after he had made the same journey in reverse—she pointed out the irony.

"It seems right that you should have made the trek down to London, Zain. After all, your dad did it for us, didn't he?"

"Yeah."

"Are you all right?"

"I'm fine, Ali." *This cannot possibly be true.*

"If you say so."

"I do. How's Glasgow?"

"The same as you left it yesterday."

Topics to avoid: Auntie Gulnar, and how long he plans to stay in London.

"All right, then," he replied.

The two remained silent for a few moments.

Zain finally broke the ice.

"So the doctor will be talking to Dad on Monday, and I want to be here for that."

"Of course, Zain. You should be."

"Thanks, babe."

"No worries. Do you need anything?"

"No, I'm all right. Cheers."

Aliseeya was trying to find a subtle way to inquire about where he might be staying, without raising the specter of his mother's house.

"Would you like me to forward your post somewhere?"

"I don't know that I'll be away long enough to warrant that, love."

"As you wish."

"Just say it, Aliseeya."

Finally.

"Whatever it is you're thinking, just say it. I can handle it."

Can you? "Very well. Have you thought about where you're going to stay?"

"Yes."

"There's no need to be pigheaded."

She knew he would hate this slur, especially during Ramadhan, even though he was not fasting.

"I'm not being that way. I kipped on the chair in Dad's room last night. I didn't want to leave his side."

"I understand, Zain. Truly, I do. I love your dad, too."

"I know. And I love that you do, after everything that's happened."

"I have no quarrels with your dad. He's amazing. I feel like he's my dad, too."

"He feels the same way about you, babes. He loves you like a daughter."

Aliseeya had lined it up at the wicket. Now she just had to bat.

"By the way, Zain, sleeping on a chair is not practical. You can't keep dossing down in a hospital."

"I've booked a hotel in Balham for tonight."

It seemed odd to her that Zain—a native Londoner like herself—should stay in a hotel when he had so many friends and family members who would gladly put him up. After a moment's reflection, his reasoning suddenly dawned on her. Zain Jaffar, proud like his mother, wouldn't want to draw attention to the family drama.

Oh no, Zain. I will not let you stay in some God-forsaken hotel.

"Right, then. You're staying with my mum. I'm texting her now."

Zain went silent. His instinct was to refuse the generous offer, but he knew better than to disagree with Aliseeya. He never wanted to find himself on the wrong side of a Justice woman.

It was a genius tactical stroke on Aliseeya's part. Zain knew that refusing to stay with Damaris would cause great offense.

Zain may have seen Gulnar in the hospital, but the two said very little to each other. All the same, he didn't want to provoke his mother. He could only imagine how she would react when she learned that he was staying with Damaris. But he had no choice. Aliseeya had outmaneuvered him.

Chapter 26

The following Monday, Anil, Gulnar, and Zain met with a cardiologist. She informed them that Anil's heart attack had been severe—three arteries were discovered to have been almost entirely blocked. Surgeons would need to insert stents into his arteries. They would operate on Anil on Wednesday and release him on Friday. Zain would settle his father at home and head back to Glasgow on the following bank holiday Monday.

The situation seemed manageable for Zain. He could work on some stories from London and email them to *The Herald*. His boss, Malcolm, released him for a week's compassionate leave without fuss. Gulnar's only words to her son were to inquire about his accommodations.

"Do you have a comfortable bed in the house, flat, or hotel where you are staying?"

The way her question lingered suggested that she was digging, but Zain ceded no ground.

Nice one, mother. Subtle.

"I do." *Keep it cool, Zain. Keep it cool.*

"And you do have decent food to eat?"

Could it be that his father really hadn't told her where he was staying? Gulnar knew Damaris was an amazing cook.

"Yes, thank you," Zain replied.

She made one final gesture.

"Zain, if there is anything you would like from the house, from your old bedroom, I can bring it along to the hospital for you."

While the words were cordial, suggesting a mother who had accepted her son's current living arrangements, they were spoken in a tone in which she might as well have been saying, *"How could you leave me all alone at a time like this?"*

This situation was tough enough for Zain without this dose of Gulnar's dramatic flair. He found it painful to see his father in a hospital bed, and he never got used to the atmosphere of the hospital and its depressing blue walls.

Apart from being confined to his room, Anil did not seem particularly ill or weak.

"The heart is a resilient organ," had been the cardiologist's exact words. The stent insertion went well. Zain had never been so happy to see his father as he was at that moment, in the private post-operation room just outside the theatre. Gulnar uttered a prayer of thanks in Arabic, and Zain echoed it. The tiniest of smiles appeared on her face.

Anil whispered, "Zain, beta, if you want to text Aliseeya to let her know that the procedure was successful, please do."

With that pronouncement, the spell was broken. Anil beamed, Gulnar's face fell, and Zain stood like a statue, staring blankly at the blue wall.

***

The day after Anil's surgery, Zain went to visit him. Gulnar had rung her husband to inform him that she was resting at home for the day, exhausted from the week's events. Zain was glad to have the day alone with his father. The two chatted, joked, and laughed, and the younger Jaffar coaxed stories out of the elder. When he could see that his dad was tired, Zain told him he was off to the canteen, in search of a coffee.

Upon returning to find Anil sleeping soundly, Zain removed the laptop from his bag and worked on an article for *The Herald*. This quiet time with his father was his favorite part of what had been an entirely lovely day.

As Zain began packing up to leave for Damaris's house that evening, Anil whispered, "Please arrive by ten tomorrow morning. That's when the doctor is coming to talk to us."

"What does she need to talk to us about?"

"She says the surgeons have found something that concerns them."

"I'm sure it's nothing, Dad."

"Just come first thing, please, beta."

"Of course. Will do."

"I love you, son."

"I know." *What's wrong with me? Why can't I say I love you?*

Chapter 27

Time is experienced as an emotion. It can feel fast or slow. The sensation of time moving slowly can induce feelings of stagnation. Its quick pace can be exciting and dangerous. The briefest moment can upturn the course of destiny.

On that Friday morning in late May 2010, when the London rain had let up for a while, and it seemed that Zain could learn to be around Gulnar without engaging in conversation with her, time suddenly felt scarce. All his thirty-four years seemed to vanish in a flash—a cruel trick of the mind. A desperate feeling of wanting to do anything in his power to somehow grab hold of more time, took over.

The doctors had pronounced, "With treatment, you could live up to twenty-two months, Mister Jaffar."

"That's assuming the treatment is successful, yes?" Anil hadn't even flinched.

His cardiologist replied, "That is correct, sir. And we have no reason to believe that it won't go well."

The double negative in that sentence should cause alarm, Zain thought, but held his tongue.

The second doctor concurred. "That's right, Mister Jaffar. You're a relatively healthy and strong man for your age."

Zain ignored that note of optimism. He had heard everything he needed to hear.

When doctors start using the word believe, *it's over.*

The younger Jaffar man, who felt like a mere boy in that moment, held it together while the doctors talked about more tests, radiology, and chemotherapy. Their words washed over him, the details subconsciously absorbed into his mind, thanks to his obsessive attention to detail.

As soon as the doctors left Anil's room and closed the door behind them, Zain embraced his father on his side, tears streaming down his face.

Gulnar embraced her husband from the other side, and the three held each other, with Anil still maintaining his composure. Being the kind spirit that he was, Anil didn't find it troublesome that he was having to comfort his wife and son at a time when he should be expecting the reverse.

The Jaffars said very little to each other after the meeting. Zain packed up his father's belongings while his parents sat in stony silence.

Taking Anil by the arm, he walked him out of the hospital and eased him into the front seat of the car. After procuring the keys from Gulnar, Zain drove his parents to their home in Gleneagle Road, instinctively finding his way through the narrow streets without reading any signs. Not a word was uttered for the duration of the drive. Each time they were stopped at a traffic light, Anil would place his hand over Zain's and smile.

Zain texted Damaris to inform her that he would be staying with his parents that night. He organized food for Anil and Gulnar, after which he returned to his childhood bedroom, a space that been untouched for the last four years. He fell into a deep sleep, hoping against hope that the day's events had all been a bad dream.

Chapter 28

The next several months flew by. Zain's weekend trips to London never seemed to give him enough time with his father. There were a few occasions on which time seemed to slow down, such as when Zain would drive Anil to the Accidents and Emergency department, and sit with him, waiting to be seen by a doctor.

Toward the end of December, the family of three—Anil, Gulnar, and Zain—had known that Anil's condition was worsening, but they remained silent in an unspoken pact. The pact was fueled by their complicity: they were all avoiding the inevitable until they no longer could.

Zain returned to London on the Friday before Christmas—as he had been doing nearly every Friday since May—and knew, just by looking at Anil, that he was ready for a graceful exit.

We don't have a choice about when we go. But he's ready and wants to do it with love, as he has done all his life.

Escaping the chilly air of Tooting, Zain entered the hospital to find Anil looking ashen. It was like beholding a worn-out version of himself—his very own Portrait of Dorian Gray. The Jaffar men looked alike. Like his father, Zain was tall, though Anil loomed over him when the two stood side by side, both just under six feet. They shared the same caramel eyes, prominent forehead, aquiline nose, and bony limbs.

As Anil was sleeping, his toes peeked out from under the thin white blanket—an object that appeared institutional and perfunctory to Zain. He tried to cover his father's feet, but the blanket wasn't long enough.

Despite the gentle care with which Zain took this action, Anil awoke. He slowly opened his eyes, looking at Zain as if encountering a stranger, just for a moment, until he was struck by the recognition of his dear son. Zain received a smile from his dad that he knew he would never again be duplicated in the same manner.

Just then, Gulnar walked in, holding two cups.

"I've brought you a coffee, Zain."

"Thanks, Mum."

"It's cold out there, isn't it?"

"Yes, it is."

"How was your journey?"

"Uneventful. Thanks. The tube ride from Euston was more wearying than the train ride down from Glasgow."

"Naturally," she replied.

This was the most Zain had said to his mother in seven months.

After a few tortuous minutes of thinking about how to fill the silence, Zain said, "I was wondering about the temperature in here. Daddy's feet are cold."

"I'll see to it, love. You stay here while I go and fetch someone to help us with the heating. I shan't be a minute."

Zain felt bad for having said anything to Gulnar. She appeared to take it as a sign that the ice between them was thawing. It was not. He was only speaking to her because he knew the time was drawing near when he would no longer have to encounter her.

Zain sat in the chair next to the bed. For once, it was his turn to read Anil's mind. Zain divined that his dad was making a mental checklist of all the things that needed to be sorted.

"Listen, Daddy. I don't want you to worry about anything, okay?"

"Okay, beta."

"Is there anything you would like me to do for you? Anyone you would like to see?"

"Yes, you should call the mosque. Please ask them to send someone to perform the last rites."

"Sure, Dad."

Anil was so matter-of-fact with his request that Zain had no choice but to maintain his composure.

Looking around at the blue walls that surrounded him, he thought, *I'm glad she left the room. Dad would never have made that request in front of her. Lord knows that woman can produce drama like no one else, which is the last thing we need right now.*

Gulnar returned with a nurse and gestured toward her husband's feet. Upon feeling Anil's cold feet, a gloomy expression came over the nurse's face.

Zain excused himself and left the ward to call the mosque. That evening, someone arrived to perform the last rites. Anil remained calm throughout the ceremony, repeating the prayers as instructed, with grace and magnanimity. Gulnar and Zain stood on opposite sides of the bed to the pastor.

Listening to Anil ask for absolution for his misdeeds, Zain felt a tear trickle down his cheek. Gulnar touched her son's hand, but it was a bridge too far—he whisked out of the room.

As soon as he was in the corridor, Zain breathed a sigh of relief. It was good to be away from those blue walls, from his grasping mother, and from the unarticulated but audible sensation of his father's impending death.

Anil's brother and his wife walked down the hospital corridor. Zain gestured to the pastor, and his uncle entered the blue room. His aunt remained in the corridor and embraced Zain. For the first time since that grim Friday in May which had brought the bad tidings, Zain let all of his tears out. In that moment, he felt like a child, about to lose all that was most dear to him.

Chapter 29

London, 2011

Mark Duggan. Damilola Taylor. Stephen Lawrence. Orlando Justice. Black British men who passed away before their time. Of course, my Papa Justice did not die at the hands of the police like Duggan, Taylor, and Lawrence. Regardless, they all left this world too soon.

Is it wrong that I'm secretly pleased that riots have broken out here? I don't just mean because of the great shots I've been taking and getting published. Sure, I'm glad to be covering a UK story which is internationally newsworthy. More importantly, it's about time the grievances of the Afro-Caribbean community in Britain were heard loud and clear.

The Brixton Riots happened a long time ago, and I was too young to fully understand what was going on. Though, even as a child, I knew something was amiss. By trying to shelter me from everything—the riots taking place less than a mile from our house, everyday racism, the death of my papa—Mum made me the curious person I am. Dear old Damaris, with all her good intentions, could not halt the inevitable. I have been poking my nose into other people's business since my childhood, and I make no apologies for it.

Thank goodness Uncle Anil spotted my interest in photography and bought me my first Yashica. If she'd had her way, Mum would have had me become a nurse like her. Were it not for my darling Zain's dad's insistence that I possessed talent, I would not have become a photojournalist. Fortunately, no parent wants to be shown up by someone else's praise of their child, especially not a Justice woman. I remember Mum's exact words: "Of caaars our Ali has talent, Anil. She was born to capture every moment on film!"

The minute I learned that Mark Duggan had been killed by police, I knew it would all kick off. Tottenham is like Brixton—a place enmeshed in pride and poverty. It takes the death of one of their own to remind people that they are oppressed. The very tool used to lull people into complacency—consumerism—has blown up in their faces. The glass of the shop windows may have been the first to go, but what has really been shattered is the illusion that we live in a free and just society.

So here I am, sent by *The Herald* to cover the looting of a department store in Clapham, far from the heart of the action in North London. I wasn't shocked, exactly, by the extent of the damage. Broken glass. Burnt-out cars. People out in the streets, the coppers in retreat.

It was no different than this January in Cairo, or Seattle in 1999, when I was admittedly young and naive. At least I worked out that I could garner a front row seat if I photographed the mayhem. A black woman in these streets—any streets, really—is always in danger. But armed with a telephoto lens, I have observed that people treat me differently. With deference, if not reverence.

What is it about my possession of this object that opens doors? My camera is truly the best security device. Far from making me vulnerable to muggers, it is my lucky talisman. Perhaps this is due to the collective obsession we have with documenting everything. Or it might be the novelty of seeing a black face on the other side of the camera. Naomi Campbell may have been born in Streatham like I was, but the similarity ends there. This black woman does not subject herself to the glare of a camera lens.

What has shocked me here in London, not seven months after I covered the toppling of Hosni Mubarak in Egypt, is spotting the faces of middle-class boys I grew up with amongst those nicking trainers from high street shops. What makes them feel entitled to do so?

When they caught me glaring at them—covering their faces while I snapped their mugs—none of them cottoned onto the fact that it was me, Aliseeya Justice from Streatham. The Aliseeya whose mother, Damaris, had baked tangerine cakes for their birthdays. The same Damaris Justice who would pull any of these chaps out of the looting by their ears if she had found them.

Their faces seemed to communicate, *These shoes are the price I am extracting for racism.* As if stealing shoes can be considered quid pro quo for living in an unequal society.

I've seen some crazy things in my line of work, but this really takes the biscuit. I mean, come on, *shoes for racism*? Do me a favor! How about paid mortgages for racism, or funding women's shelters for racism, or buying food for homeless people for racism? Surely these would be more useful than shoes.

I could argue that my papa died because of racism. Throughout his life, the man was obsessed with doing all things British, leading right up to that fatal final supper in Wales. But you don't see me running into a shop and snatching a pair of trainers as revenge.

Poor Papa. I miss him. He always tried so hard to fit in. Personally, I don't get it. What's so special about being British, anyway? If Britain is so great, why did it have to venture all over the world and steal other people's countries? Don't they have everything they need right here in Great Britain?

I wouldn't admit this to anyone, but British politeness has been good for my career. I find that people are not just deferential when I've got my camera, tripod, and crew with me, but they are actually fearful of me. It works for me—leave me alone to do my job. I like being at the center of the action and shooting captivating photos, however dire the situation.

These London riots, however, have no redeeming qualities. The stereotypes, misperceptions, and injustices which led to the killing of Mark Duggan will only be perpetuated by the looting. You cannot get people to end their oppression of you by throwing rage in their faces. It did not work in India, Rwanda, or East Timor, and it will not work in North London.

Look at Auntie Gulnar. I'm sure she's witnessed some oppression in her time, but the way she is carrying on is not helping her case. Zain doesn't see it this way. But then, which child is ever rational when it comes to their mother? I know I'm not. Damaris drives me dotty, but I wouldn't want anyone else for my mum. After all, she raised me with the maxim, *"Remember, Aliseeya, everybody is bredren."*

God, I love her. Zain loves his mother, too, but he doesn't think I could handle it if he admitted that to me. Lord knows the woman needs help. And as my sainted mother says, *"I've never met a problem I couldn't knock on its head."*

She's right. When people were sad, or celebrating, or just in need of reminding that someone cared, Mum would put together a care package for them. I think Zain's mum is in need of just such attention. After all, she's lost not only a husband, but also a son—in my name, no less—though I have no quarrel with her.

There's no talking to Zain, who simply throws up his grief as a shield. If I tell him that the potatoes are undercooked, he'll say, "Well, I'm grieving, you know."

Blimey! How do I respond to that? *"You know, darling, that I'm very sorry for the loss of your father. I also loved him like a father since my own dad died when I was ten. Yes, I'm okay, although thinking about Orlando and Anil makes me sad. But could you please leave the spuds to boil on the hob for another ten minutes?"*

I think not. There's no telling him. Silence is a disease spreading across our household, into the heart of our relationship. So I just sit there and sigh, waiting for my next out-of-town assignment. The irony is that Zain also takes exception to my silence.

Out of nowhere, he'll ask, "What?"

"Nothing."

"I know something's bothering you," he'll say, in perfect imitation of his father.

"It's nothing worth worrying yourself over, sweetie."

Men are so simple. Zain will accept my placating sentiments, which is markedly different from his dad. Uncle Anil would have gently persisted until he identified the problem, and then talked it through it until it was resolved.

Oh, those lovely Jaffar men! Zain and his dad were cut from the same cloth, but it didn't stretch out long enough in the younger man's case. He has all the conviction and none of the finesse of Uncle Anil.

Zain is basically a good egg, though. My thirty-plus years of knowing him confirms this, and I do love him. I can see his flaws, and yet not want to throw away what we have and all that we've built together. If only the good people of India, Rwanda, and East Timor could have extended their hearts in this way, things might have turned out differently for them. There is still hope for the good people of North London.

Chapter 30

When I was growing up, Mum used to litter every conversation with Jamaican proverbs such as, *When cocoa is ripe, it must bust.* Meaning, actions speak louder than words.

Good old Damaris never put up with any of my complaints. If I informed her that some object was broken, she would say, "Why you a come to me? The Lord gave you two hands."

If I went to her express my unhappiness about a situation, she would listen patiently, give me a hug, and ask, "So watchu going to do about it, Ali baby?"

Ever since Uncle Anil died last year, I have been unhappy about the discomfited dynamic between Zain, his mother, and myself. So in true Damaris Justice fashion, I assembled a care package for Auntie Gulnar, including the following: my mum's delectable homemade tangerine cake, a paperback edition of Chinua Achebe's *Things Fall Apart,* Miriam Makeba's *Africa* album, and a bottle of aspirin.

I attached a note to the package.

Dear Mrs. Jaffar,

As Franz Kafka once beseeched: "Don't despair, not even over the fact that you don't despair. Just when everything seems over with, new forces come marching up, and precisely that means you are alive. And if they don't, then everything is over here, for once and for all."

I left the card unsigned. I'm certain that Gulnar would not be pleased to see my name. In any case, she should recognize my handwriting, or surmise that I am the giver of this unexpected gift. Who else would deliver a tangerine cake so recognizably baked by my mum?

Definitely not Damaris Justice herself. She is still smarting from the perceived injury inflicted on me by Auntie Gulnar. In this case, Mum is not following her own maxim to always take action.

I can't blame her for letting things fester. Although the two women were like sisters for decades, it appears that Auntie Gulnar is going out of her way to alienate everyone. The last time I saw her—at Uncle Anil's funeral—she was super awkward, not even making eye contact with Zain.

My mum loves the bones of Zain. She would do anything for him. I think she might love him more than me. Or at least, is more protective of him because of his vulnerability. Ask her to go anywhere near Gulnar Jaffar, however, and she will proclaim, "Pickney, I wouldn't touch that lady with a barge pole!"

The Justice and Jaffar women: stubborn as ever, both. That's why it's up to me to try to fix our family dynamic, even if I felt like a spy when dropping off the package. I thought about using a courier service, but settled on delivering it in person because I wanted to see the old house where Zain grew up. I know he misses the place, and he'll never admit it.

I was avoiding Gleneagle Road until recently, even though it's just around the corner from Mum's street. I especially wanted to see it because I've not been there since Uncle Anil passed away, and I still associate the house with him, right down to the rickety steps leading to the front door, and the weed-ridden garden. I'm happy that some things never change.

Uncle Anil was that rare person who recognized the beauty of the human spirit, but cared not a jot for the less significant things in life, like trimming the hedges and mending the broken fixtures around the house.

Auntie Gulnar is a different kettle of fish. Put a tea towel out of place in her presence, and Lord have mercy, you would never hear the end of it. I don't know how those two survived nearly forty years of marriage. But then again, she loves to talk, and he was a good listener. Perhaps a lot of her guff went in one of his big hairy ears and out the other one.

I can observe the same thing already starting to happen with me and Zain. Sometimes he'll repeat a word I've said and look at me like I've just spoken Swahili. Only last week, we were sitting down to dinner, and I wanted to make sure we had all the crockery.

"Did you fetch the salad plates, love?"

Zain stared at me blankly. After a moment, he realized that he had missed what I'd said, so he asked, "Sorry Aliseeya, what was that?"

"The salad plates, Zain."

"Salad plates?" He was looking at me as if I had asked for Portuguese Men of War.

"Yes, the little round plates on which we place a few tired leaves of lettuce and sundry veg."

"Oh, the *salad plates*. Got it. Right away." And off he went to the kitchen.

Thirty-four is far too young for him to be going dotty. And let's face it, the family track record is not good. Poor Auntie Gulnar. That, however, is a topic on which Zain refuses to engage at all. At that same dinner, once the salad plates were located, I attempted a gentle start.

"Zain, I'm worried about your mum. How is she coping all by herself in that rickety old house?"

"Oh, she'll be fine, I'm sure."

"That's just it. You *don't* know. You've cut off all communication, but I know you still care about her."

Rather than acknowledging that he did indeed care—or denying it—Zain launched into a diatribe.

"Let me remind you that I am not speaking to her because of her treatment of you."

"Much appreciated."

"Oi! Are you being sarky with me, Aliseeya?"

"Uh, no. I genuinely appreciate your standing up for me—for us—the way you did."

"Good."

I had him right where I wanted him.

Just as he was settling into his smugness, I retorted, "And now that we've sorted that bit out, I'd like to point out that not once did I ask you to stop talking to your mum for my sake."

He looked like a boy who's just had his ice lolly snatched.

"But I—"

"Let me stop you right there. It was a noble gesture, to be sure. But now that your dad's gone, I think we ought to show your mum a little more compassion, even if she has not extended the same courtesy to us. She is a human being, after all. I still care about her, despite everything she's said and done, and I know you do, too. Our two families share a long history."

Top that, I thought.

Zain didn't come back with anything. How could he? What argument can be made against treating someone—even one who has harmed you—with a little kindness? Without such consideration, humanity is doomed.

Getting up from the table in a huff, Zain marched out of the flat.

He mumbled, "I need a little air," and stormed off into the dark Glaswegian evening.

I have never been one to miss an opportunity in life, especially when armed with my camera. Indeed, I owe my career to that famous moment when I captured Tony Blair's awkward goofy-toothed grin at the Gleneagles Summit precisely when he thought no one was looking. Similarly, I decided to use Zain's lack of a retort as his implicit agreement that it was time for an entente with Auntie Gulnar. Hence, the idea of a gift to show our goodwill. What can he possibly say about a simple care package? Surely not this: *"I do not want you to be kind to my mother, because I feel injured by her on your behalf."* That's hardly likely to come out of his mouth. If I'm willing to travel to her London home just to deliver her a cake and some trinkets, I've obviously moved on. Zain simply cannot go on milking this situation for drama. It's time for my man to turn over a new leaf.

Chapter 31

That Saturday evening, Damaris drove Aliseeya to Gulnar's house, bearing the tangerine cake in a box embossed with a red hibiscus pattern, and the gifts in a bag. Damaris had always said, *"You can't go wrong with red, child. 'Tis a color that'll make people sit up and take notice."*

As a photographer, Aliseeya placed more importance on observing others than on being noticed herself, which was why she favored a monochromatic wardrobe. On this occasion, however, she wanted her peace offering for Gulnar to be striking in every way.

Damaris admired her daughter's determination in seeking out a Jaffar–Justice reconciliation. She was thus insistent that Aliseeya present the gifts in showy packaging.

"Pickney! You can't just go and give someone a tangerine cake in a raggedy old box now. You hear what me say?"

Aliseeya loved when her mum broke out into Patois. Damaris knew this, and used her charming verbiage to command her daughter about the etiquette of gift-giving, and the importance of tangerine cakes. And it was no trouble—Damaris always stored floral-patterned boxes under her roomy staircase for just this sort of occasion.

The car ride transported Aliseeya back to her childhood, when she would frequently be dropped off at her friend Zain's house for an afternoon of play.

Now, while Damaris waited in the street with the motor running, Aliseeya strolled up the footpath and placed the heavy cake box on the front porch, along with a cloth bag containing the novel, album, aspirin, and the handwritten note.

Out of nowhere—for Aliseeya had not spotted any lights or movement in the house—the door opened, revealing an amazed Gulnar Jaffar, who said, "Hello, darling! Is it really you? My word! Fancy seeing you after all this time. You simply must come in. Is that your mother I see there waiting in the motor car? Won't you please ask her to come in and join us for a spot of tea?"

Aliseeya was taken aback by Gulnar's warmth. They hadn't spoken for five years, and had barely acknowledged each other at Anil's funeral the previous year. Aliseeya had hoped that her peace offering would lead to a gradual thawing of their relationship, but Gulnar's ostentatious outburst of cordiality was entirely unexpected.

Aliseeya felt she had no choice but to accept the invitation to come in for tea. Gesturing to Damaris to join her, Aliseeya entered the house, which looked as immaculate as ever, but was scented with the air of widowhood.

Over tea and tangerine cake, Gulnar regaled the Justice women with fanciful tales of Dar es Salaam, lingering over the episode of her private audience with Maria Nyerere. She held court all evening while declining to refer to Damaris or Aliseeya by name, and making no mention of her son or dead husband. It seemed to Aliseeya that Gulnar Jaffar was in complete denial about everything.

The next day, Aliseeya returned to Glasgow, feeling ecstatic. She waited until dinnertime to share the news with Zain, knowing he would need time to process it. After the meal, she recounted everything to him: her idea for the care package, Damaris's assistance, Gulnar's friendly welcome, and the ladies' teatime conversation. Zain sat stony-faced.

Following her excited account, the first thing he blurted out was, "That's all well and good, but she's still a racist, Ali."

Aliseeya took a deep breath and launched into a diatribe.

"You do know that your mother is not personally responsible for all the actions of colonial invaders in Tanzania, don't you? You're living in a dream world with your fanciful ideas and righteous judgements. I certainly don't need schooling on racism from you, Zainy! Do you want to know what everyday racism feels like? This one time, I went to a club in Berlin to see a well-known folk singer. When I paid the entry fee, the bouncer stamped a happy face on my hand. During the gig, I felt my mobile vibrating. Seeing that it was my manager, I ran outside to take the call. When I was finished, the woman on the door wouldn't let me back in because she couldn't see the happy face stamp on my dark skin. So I don't need *you* to preach to me about racism, mate! I know it. I live with it every day. At the same time, I don't get stuck in it. I keep on moving. Enough already with your idealistic notions. This is your mum we're talking about, for Chrissake!"

Following her speech, Zain stared blankly at Aliseeya, sitting silently for a long time—a phenomenon she had observed in him with alarmingly increased frequency since Anil had died.

Then he shrugged. "Fine."

Zain still wished for an apology from his mother following her reaction to the news of their relationship five years prior. However, he could not deny that Gulnar inviting Aliseeya and Damaris to tea was a positive development.

Regardless of his issues with his mum, he felt carried along by the tide of events that had been started by Aliseeya's peace offering. If the Justice and Jaffar families were not yet fully reconciled, the ice had been broken, thanks to Aliseeya's thoughtful gifts, including Damaris's tangerine cake.

Chapter 32

London, 2011

My Dear Zain,

The vultures are circling. I recently received a gift of Chinua Achebe's *Things Fall Apart* on my doorstep. It put me in mind of Joni Mitchell's "Slouching Towards Bethlehem," in which she alludes to Yeats's poem *The Second Coming*.

> *Turning and turning*
> *With the widening gyre,*
> *The falcon cannot hear the falconer.*
> *Things fall apart.*
> *The center cannot hold,*
> *And a blood dimmed tide*
> *Is loosed upon the world.*

I do not know where to go or what to do, son. I have some shocking news. I received a visit from the woman who has been haunting me all these years. Yes, it was none other than the redoubtable Maria Nyerere herself, accompanied by her daughter, who is a tall, lean, and glamorous woman with shortly cropped hair.

The two ladies came to the front door of our house, right here in Streatham! Can you believe it, darling? That crafty Mrs. Nyerere finally tracked me down, just as I always feared she would. It all happened so quickly. I heard some rustling in the front garden, and so I walked to the doorway and could just make out the silhouette of the younger Ms. Nyerere through the frosted glass of the alcove window.

That tall woman was setting down a box—it was very gaudy, covered in a pattern of red hibiscus flowers—containing a tangerine cake, and a bag containing a book, a record, and some pills in a bottle. They must think I

am stupid if they imagine that I will swallow those tablets. Let's face it, if
I did, that would be the end of your mother—*kaput, khalas, kwisha kabisa*!
    There was commotion in Gleneagle Road. The neighbors were starting
to peer out from behind their lace curtains. I saw the focus of their attention. It was none other than the stately Maria Nyerere sitting in the driver's
seat of a panda car! I don't believe that woman ever touched a doorknob
in Tanzania, let alone a steering wheel. And there she was, the former first
lady, sitting in a rubbish motor car and glaring at me, cool as a cucumber.
    Given our longstanding acquaintance, I had no choice but to invite her
in, along with the tall, lean glamour-puss at my door, who I deduced must
be Maria's daughter, given the resemblance. I had to fake my enthusiasm.
    "How lovely to see you! Won't you and your mother please come in
for a spot of tea?"
    "Thank you, Missus Jaffar. I will go and ask her. I shan't be a minute."
    Maria must have told her my name, for I had never been introduced
to any of the Nyerere children. And just like that, I was entertaining the
former first lady of Tanzania and her glamorous-looking daughter, in our
humble front parlor. I was livid—how dare they force themselves upon me!
It felt as if they were paying a charitable visit on a lonely widow, out of a
sense of *noblesse oblige*. Do they think I need their pity?
    I wasted no time in reminding Mrs. Nyerere that we took afternoon
tea in her grand Ikulu in Dar es Salaam, more than four decades ago. I was
even so bold as to mention the memorable yellow fabric with yellow stars
and white starfish that covered a side table in the Palm Room. I didn't go
so far as to say that I knew she had it copied from my dress material, but I
think she understood my inference. For she had a strange, furtive look in
her eyes.

Chapter 33

Glasgow, 2011

Everywhere I have traveled as a photojournalist, I have encountered people who are constantly looking, but see nothing. I am certainly guilty of being a gazer, especially through the camera lens. But I would like to think that I also engage my other senses. These days, I find that people don't hear properly, as they're listening to everything through earbuds. They taste the same commoditized airport lounge food everywhere in the world. And as for smell…I can't go there.

But the most important lesson I've learned is how to be an empath. My Zain is such a compassionate man, but he has an immovable block when it comes to his mother. I thought that things might change after his father's passing, and especially last week, after Auntie Gulnar welcomed Mum and me into her home for tea. That meeting did slowly begin the process of thawing the ice, but Zain remains unwilling to admit that he might have been wrong about her. I understand. After all, it can't be easy to step back from having labeled your mother a racist, and instead suspect that she's gone barmy.

I always felt that I was partly a political cause for Zain. I know that he loves me. But relationships are built on so much more than love. On top of that core foundation are all the other elements. All of the time, support, and energy that Zain has invested in us were influenced not just by who I am, but also what I represent.

Not that I mind this entirely. I know there are others who would avoid me because of what I represent. I photograph such people every day. At the same time, it's not easy when one of the pillars of your relationship is your boyfriend's desire to prove a point to his mother.

After all we've been through, I no longer care about proving a point, or being right. Zain, on the other hand, has become recalcitrant in his position, and will not be moved when it comes to his mother.

Chapter 34

Glasgow, 2011

On a balmy Glaswegian evening—when the light was at its best, just before the twilight hour in that spirited Caledonian city—Zain decided he would finally have it out with Aliseeya.

Enough is enough, he thought. *This has gone too far.*

As soon as she entered the flat—fresh from her most recent assignment covering the fallout from the London riots—he gently requested that she sit down.

"Darling, we need to talk."

"Whoa. Those are five words no woman wants to hear."

"I don't know what you mean."

"Well, I know what *you* mean. You want to split up with me."

"Blimey, no! How could you possibly deduce that from what I said?"

"Well, you said, 'Darling, we need to talk.'"

"What's wrong with that?"

"You never call me darling, so I'm immediately suspicious."

Zain just glared while Aliseeya continued.

"Plus, I find it odd that you would say, 'we need to talk,' when we're already talking. I mean, there's talking, and then there's *talking*. Clearly, there's a problem."

"Yes, there is a problem, but it's nothing to do with us. It's my mother."

"Oh no! Is Auntie Gulnar okay?"

"I don't know. See for yourself."

He handed her Gulnar's letter describing the visit from Maria Nyerere and her daughter, bearing various gifts, including a tangerine cake.

After reading it, Aliseeya was silent—a rare occurrence. Zain couldn't bring himself to tell her about the volumes of letters he had been receiving for months.

His mind went straight to the worst possibility.

"I'm sorry to ask this, Aliseeya, but what the devil did you and Auntie Damaris get up to when you visited my mum?"

"What do you mean, *what did we get up to*? We went to deliver a care package, and she invited us in for tea."

"Do you have any reason to believe that she might not have recognized you two?"

"I suppose that's possible. Wait, you're not suggesting that Mum and I passed ourselves off as the Nyerere women, are you? I had never even heard that name until last week."

"What else could it be?"

"I don't have to sit here and listen to this!"

"Be reasonable, babe. I'm at my wit's end."

"Don't you *babe* me."

"Aliseeya."

"Zain. You listen to me. If you don't like what I have to say, you can take a long running jump. I'm at my wit's end, too."

"I'm all ears."

"Your mother is not a well woman. The entire time we were together, she refused to address us by name, or ask us how we were. All she did was recount the story of her visit with the first lady at the Tanzanian State House. It's as though she's obsessed."

"Yikes."

"There's more. She made no reference to you or your dad, and all photos of the three of you have been removed. Something is seriously wrong with her."

"Maybe she's still grieving and doesn't want to be reminded of how much she misses my dad."

"You know, what Z? Your wishful thinking is almost as scary as Auntie Gulnar's behavior. I mean, what kind of wicked people would my mum and I be not to correct her if we knew she had mistaken us for the Nyereres?"

"You're right. I'm sorry, Aliseeya. I guess I just don't want to believe that she's lost the plot."

"I don't blame you. It can't be easy."

"Nope."

"Don't look so forlorn, Z. We're in this together."

"I appreciate that."

"Of course. We're family. We've already been through a lot. We both lost our fathers. Your dad loved me like a daughter. My mum loves you like a son. Surely we can get through this."

"Can we?"

"What choice do we have? We're not going to just ignore your mum, especially if she's dotty."

"I just…I just wish…it's moments like this when I really miss my dad."

"I know. I miss him, too."

"Plus, she was fine while he was alive. How did she suddenly flip a switch?"

"I don't know, love. All I know is that right now, she really needs us. She could be a danger to herself."

"Do you think so?"

"I do. I mean, how can she not recognize people she's known as family for over thirty years? Do me a favor."

"Go on."

"Maybe I'm wrong about your mum. I suppose it's possible that she is perfectly sane, and just playing some twisted psychological game designed to reel you in."

"What? That's mad!"

"It could be worse."

"How so?"

"Well, she might be having a breakdown. The warmth with which she greeted us cannot be faked. She was genuinely grateful for our company, but she seemed confused."

Chapter 35

Aliseeya and Zain agreed that they should act immediately to make sure that Gulnar was okay. Even if they left Glasgow straight away—which they could not, due to their work commitments—they would reach London in five hours on the train. The flight was only an hour, not counting the time it took to check in, proceed through the security, and travel to and from the airport.

Instead, they decided to ring Aliseeya's mum and ask her to drive around and look in on Gulnar. After all, in addition to being a trusted family friend, Damaris worked as a nurse, and she might be able to intervene if it came to the worst.

Damaris reported to Aliseeya that Gulnar seemed fine, and that the two women had a lovely chat in the doorway. Although, this time, an invitation to take tea was not extended. The only observation from Damaris which spooked them was that she could spot a suitcase near the stairway, though Gulnar had done her best to block it from view, hurrying Damaris off and telling her to come back another time.

Gulnar had said, "I'm fine, you understand, sister. Nothing to worry about. Just a little tiredness."

Damaris quoted these words to Aliseeya on the phone.

"Nothing else, Mum?"

"No, pickney! I did what you kids asked, and went over there as promised. But I cannot exactly push my way into that sistren's house, can I?"

"Auntie Gulnar didn't offer any clue as to where she might be headed?"

"No. But now that you ask, she said something strange at the end of our conversation, about how I must miss Kenya. I corrected her and said Jamaica. Then she winked at me. 'Twas very strange and sad to see tings come to such a pretty pass for me dear old friend."

Following this report, Zain rang the landline of the Jaffar home for the first time since his father's heart attack over a year ago, but there was no answer. Scared about what Gulnar might do, or where she might go, Zain and Aliseeya made the train journey down to London that Friday, his first since Anil had passed away.

Upon entering Gulnar's house, Zain and Aliseeya found a note from her on the hall table.

My Dear Zain,

Yes, I have fled, but you mustn't worry about me. And for heaven's sake, please don't start a wild goose chase, foolishly trying to track down your mother. I am fine. More than fine, in fact. For if you are reading this, it means you have come home, and that you still love me. I am happy with that knowledge alone, even if I lose everything else.

I had the strangest visitor here on Gleneagle Road. This time it was in Maria Nyerere, but Margaret Kenyatta. Of course, I cannot deny our family connection to her. Your father's cousin Nasim was acquainted with her when she was known as Margaret Gakuo. She and Nasim were classmates at St. Andrew's boarding school near Nakuru. Why Mrs. Kenyatta should seek me out, God only knows. While I did attend Nairobi's High Ridge Teachers College, I was never embroiled in Kenyan politics. Tanzania is a different story, but you already know that.

Mrs. Kenyatta came here, right to the door through which you have just entered. I tell you, son, I have had enough of these hoity-toity ladies! Why must they obsess over me? I was merely a Dar es Salaam glamour girl who was tasked with subtly schooling Mrs. Nyerere on teatime etiquette. Just one afternoon tea with Maria, on behalf of the Women's Association, and my whole life gets turned upside down.

I must admit that Mrs. Kenyatta was beautiful. Striking. She looked solid and sturdy, ready to withstand a hurricane. And she smelled as though she had emerged from a bakery with tangerines in it. What lady in her right mind goes around scented like a citrus fruit?

She said, "Hello, Gulnar. I wanted to check on you, as my daughter and her boyfriend are concerned about you."

I cannot believe that woman had the cheek to address me by my first name! What was I to think? We had never met before, and there she was at my front door, smelling tangerine-fresh and nattering about her daughter's concerns. What in the world do Margaret Kenyatta's daughter and her boyfriend have to do with me?

I'm ashamed to admit that, for the first time in my life, I was not a hospitable hostess. I did not offer tea, or even a glass of water, to Margaret, who must have traveled from Palace Gate, Kensington, where I believe the Kenyatta family occupies a grand home. I am no longer in the right humor to entertain, Zain. The poor woman left without anything to eat or drink. It's just as well, for I am not good company right now.

Come to think of it, she is not a poor woman at all. These families have already taken enough from Africa. I wasn't going to let them pull one over on me too!

It's got to the point where I can't even drink tea in my own house without thinking about these elegant ladies who have finally tracked me down after all these years. Like vultures, they were waiting for your father to go so that they could swoop down on me. I cannot bear it any longer, so I am leaving. I shall not tell you where I am going until I have arrived there safely, and thus foreclosed the possibility of the Nyereres and the Kenyattas finding me. Who knows what they are capable of doing? After all, they have already trekked all the way to Streatham.

One more thing: be a good boy, and please thank Aliseeya for her thoughtful gift of Miriam Makeba's Mama Africa. *Just after the Nyereres descended upon me, I found the record in a bag, with a note in what can only be that darling girl's handwriting. She had written out a lovely quote from Kafka, about not despairing.*

Your Aliseeya Justice is a dear, just like her mother. I miss my lovely friend Damaris. I'm so happy that you and Aliseeya have each other. I can sleep at night, knowing that you are not alone, and that you have someone who loves you almost as much as I do. I know she will take care of you. And believe me, you need taking care of.

You are exactly like your father. Like you, he inhabited a dream world that didn't exist. I don't mean to disparage you, Zain. I just worry about you. You'll never know the lengths I have gone to just to ensure your safety. I hope that you never let go of Aliseeya. If you do, it will be the end of you. Your existence is more precarious than you realize, darling.

On a happier note, Miriam Makeba's voice on the record player brought me such joy, even as I found myself forced to leave my own home. There's no facility for playing records where I'm going, so the album is yours, as is everything I own, ultimately. Not just yet, God willing. There's some life left in your old mother yet.

Makeba's version of "Malaika" rekindled such blissful feelings in me. I remember my mother singing the refrain to me, your father singing it to me, and me singing it to you.

Malaika, nakupenda, malaika—my angel, I love you, my angel.

So Zain, I am in danger, but I love you. I always have, and always will. Please don't forget that. I love Aliseeya, too. I know that one can never correct the wrongs of the past, but I do love you both, my children, as I love my beautiful Dar es Salaam—always and forever.

Your loving mother,

Gulnar Jaffar (neé Kassam)

Chapter 36

Dar es Salaam, 2011

After forty years of discontented living in Great Britain, Gulnar Jaffar had finally found peace. Not on that cold, emotionally stilted island, but in her native Dar es Salaam.

It had been easier to return than she had expected—the barriers being primarily mental rather than substantial. All that was required was a flying visit to the passport office on Petty France for their premium passport delivery service, a journey back to Streatham to collect her case, and a taxi ride to Gatwick Airport.

The sudden drama of her departure made Gulnar feel heady. She had purchased a reasonably priced flight to Dar via Amsterdam from the airline ticket counter. After one final call to a friend, she departed, erasing not just the distance of seventy-five hundred kilometers between London and Dar es Salaam, but also four decades of yearning.

On the flights, she slept more peacefully than she had in years. Being woken to the sound of an airline steward announcing his greeting was music to her ears.

"Ladies and gentlemen, Karibuni Tanzania."

The instant Gulnar marched down the metal stairway of the aircraft and set her feet onto the tarmac, she breathed in the smoky, salty Tanzanian air and felt whole again. The heat had an unusually dry quality about it, but it was all-enveloping—a sort of humidity without moisture. For the first time since leaving this glorious place, she did not feel inclined to complain.

Even the immigration officer was kind, welcoming her home rather than chastising her for failing to obtain a visa in advance, and letting her through like a Tanzanian national owing to the place of birth on her passport.

My passport is irrelevant. My nationality is irrelevant. Everything is irrelevant. Only Zain matters.

Gulnar placed her passport back into the Chanel purse she used when traveling, and walked through the airport terminal. *I'm trying to make things right, just like Joni Mitchell in "Slouching Towards Bethlehem."*

Hoping and hoping
As if by my weak faith
The spirit of this world
Would heal and rise.

Like the immigration officer, Gulnar's taxi driver welcomed her warmly. As the driver pulled out of the airport complex, she immediately recognized the large artery bisecting the city. It had changed considerably. The Morogoro Road looked shabby-chic, without the chic. Where it had once been lined with smart boutiques and bougainvillea flowers of all colors, it was now dominated by a succession of tired palm trees, *dukas*—stores, and *dhobis*—laundromats.

Gulnar beheld her countrymen with contentedness. She witnessed old people, young people, teenagers, children, and animals, all trudging alongside the baking-hot Morogoro Road. Her fellow Tanzanians who occupied the pavements appeared to be carrying the weight of the world on their shoulders. Dar es Salaam was not the happy, carefree place she remembered.

Cry the beloved country. Life has taken a toll on us all. Joni was right:

Things fall apart.
The center cannot hold.

En route to Oyster Bay, where she had booked a hotel, Gulnar asked the driver to stop at the Kariakoo Market, near the Mnazi Mmoja Hospital, where she had been born. She wanted to buy the beautiful kanga materials which were only available here, along with some coconutty vitumbwa to munch on, and one very important item intended for a child.

By the time Gulnar had unpacked her case and walked out of the hotel lobby, she was the very picture of glamour, donning a simple white pintucked blouse, coupled with an A-line lemon chiffon skirt, and her best Ferragamo flats. On her head she bore an enormous domed straw hat which resembled something that might be worn at the fish market in Pacao, or in a paddy field in Karnataka.

On her bronzed face—which still appeared fresh after a full day of travel, thanks to her gold-flecked moisturizer—she donned a pair of tortoiseshell Alain Mikli sunglasses made especially for her by the designer. She remembered meeting Mikli and the other hoi polloi at some fashionable event.

> *None of that matters anymore. My modeling career is over. Now, I am just a mother—the most important job I've ever had.*

One of the kangas she had purchased in Kariakoo—made of a solid black fabric patterned with crooked white lines and purple spheres—was draped elegantly over her shoulders. The other one was in her enormous Dior handbag, wrapped around the precious object meant for a child. That second kanga was colored Persian blue, bearing a pattern of white lilies, and featuring an imprinted Swahili proverb. *Dawa ya moto ni moto*—The remedy for fire is fire.

As Gulnar took a luxuriant stroll toward the beach, she felt that this was the moment for which she had been waiting all those years in London, far away from her truest self. Although her husband had been passionate about politics in Tanzania—particularly in aid of advancing its people—Anil hadn't shared her sheer love of Dar, the city by the sea. He would much rather be attending a meeting of Marxists in Bloomsbury than eating roasted *macay* in Kivukoni.

> *Of course it's different for me. This love is in my blood.*

As soon as she placed her foot onto the powdery white sand, which felt like a fine flour, Gulnar wanted time to stand still. In a way, it had. She reveled in the moment, unperturbed by anything—the burning sun on her arms, the miniature pinecones crunching under her feet, the pain of losing Anil, or her guilt about the way she had fled London, leaving her vulnerable son alone, without directly sharing her whereabouts with him.

Zain would find out soon enough. *If he hasn't already worked it out, he's not much of an investigative journalist, is he?*

> *No. Don't be unkind, Gully, it's not who you are. You love that boy. You always have. Why else would you have trekked all the way to Dar?*

Bravely taking off her Ferragamos and leaving them to one side—for they were capable of walking, even when not adorning her dainty feet—Gulnar stepped into the clear, gleaming Indian Ocean. She was aware of the tiny biting fish, the bits of coral which could cut her heals, and the distant threat of sharks, but she remained blissfully oblivious to everything. From her

Dior bag, she removed the blue and white kanga which directed her to cure fire with fire, and cradled the precious cargo meant for a child in her arms.

Chapter 37

F alling in and out of sleep on his Kenyan Airways flight from London to Nairobi, where he would change for a Precision Airways flight to Dar es Salaam, Zain thought about the fateful phone call he had received before his departure.

He and Aliseeya had been frantically searching the Jaffar house for any clue which might reveal his mother's whereabouts. While Aliseeya was upstairs combing through the study, the landline rang. Gulnar still kept a telephone on a table in the front hall, as she had done since she had moved into the house in 1974.

After lifting it from its cradle, Zain answered.

"Mum? Where are you?" *I am not amused.*

"Oh no. Sorry, beta. This is not your mummy."

"Oh. All right then." Zain's taciturn nature immediately induced his silent setting.

"Hello? Beta?"

"Yes."

"Is that Zain Jaffar?"

"It is."

"Don't you wish to know to whom you are speaking, beta?"

"Sure."

"You're not a very curious boy, are you, dear? I remember you as a studious little fellow."

Who is this muppet? "Do I know you?"

"Yes. But you may not remember me. You came to my house when you were five or six years old, before I moved to Northampton. I used to live in Streatham, near you."

"I see. So what is this all about? Are you involved in my mum's caper?" *I'm being played like a violin.*

"No, no. Not at all, dear. Your mummy simply asked me to convey a message to you. I am her friend, Auntie Zainul. We used to teach together at the Aga Khan School in Dar es Salaam."

"Okay."

"Is that all you have to say? I fear your mother could be in trouble, darling."

"What do you want me to say? You hold all the cards."

"Now, now, Zainy. Please stay calm. I'm just as much in the dark as you are, beta. I don't know why Gulnar has mixed me up in this ridiculous *kichro*. I am on *your* side, dear boy. Did you know that you were named after me?"

"I did not. Mum has never mentioned you."

"That makes sense. We were very close at one time, but she has never visited me since I moved to Northampton. She always used to say, 'Who wants to go to Northampton? *Sao* jungle *jero ai*! I'd be better off in the Serengeti.'"

"That sounds like my sardonic mare of a mother."

"Besharam chokro!"

"I don't understand what you are saying."

"I called you a shameless boy! How can you declare your own mother a mare?"

"Oh, please. You know how she is. It doesn't even sound like she's been a good friend to you, auntie."

"No, no, that is not what I'm saying, beta. You must understand. Gully is a kind, loving person. I just think she has been off since your daddy went."

At that moment, Aliseeya came down the stairs and mouthed, *Who is it?*

Zain swatted her away with a dismissive hand gesture.

"Hello, beta. Are you still there, Zainy?"

"Yes, I am, Auntie Zainul. Please don't call me Zainy."

"It was said with affection, my dear. You really were named after me. Zainul—which can be either a boy's name or a girl's name—means *the best*. Our name comes from Zain Al-Abideen, Imam Ali's grandson."

Zain was reaching his limit. *This woman clearly has no one to talk to.*

"Well, you learn something new every day, don't you?" he said.

"Arré! You are speaking sarcastically to your auntie, you cheeky boy?"

"Not at all. Just discovering one more thing my mother has kept from me all these years."

"Ah. Well, discover this too. Your mother has fled to Dar. She mentioned something about returning Nyerere's grandchild to its roots, but I couldn't understand her *bakwaas*. I have fulfilled my duty. Bas! Happy now? Mad family, the lot of you." She hung up.

"Blast that confounding woman!" Zain yelled into the receiver.

Chapter 38

My Dear Aliseeya,

Greetings from beautiful Dar es Salaam, the abode of peace—a place which lives up to its lofty name in every way.

Before I go any further, let me first apologize. I never meant to hurt you, or to convey my disapproval of your relationship with Zain, on the grounds of any racialist issue, or any other animus. I solemnly swear to you, this was never the case. Far from it, as you will see when I reveal all momentarily.

This morning, I visited the Aga Khan Mzizima School, of which I was once head teacher. The warm welcome extended to me by the school's staff awoke feelings which have been lying dormant in me for years. Most especially, the *askari*—security guard—was very kind. Talking to him took me back to my childhood, growing up with Ramzani, an elder gentleman who worked as my father's driver, and Shabani, a young man who worked in the house with my mother. Ramzani was an older brother to me, and Shabani a younger one.

We used to laugh, talk, eat, go for walks, and so much more. I spent more time with these two gentlemen than with my biological brothers. Not out of condescension, guilt, or pity. Not only did we love each other, but they recognized me as one of them. You see, Aliseeya, my father's mother—no one knows her name, for unfortunately, that is how history has deigned to broach a woman in her position—was African, born and raised.

Please do not tell Zain about this. He will only mount himself higher on his ridiculously high horse. That boy has such a cut and dry sense of justice. I don't know from where he inherited it. For, as you know, my late husband, Anil, was nuanced in his approach to everything, sometimes to a tiresome degree. My Zain, on the other hand, is special. I am not warning you off. Nor am I suggesting that I love him any less because of his ways. I'm sure you have observed Zain being so obsessed with doing the right thing that he sometimes tramples on people. I know you will understand this, my daughter, if I may be so bold as to address you in this way. For I have always thought of you as such.

You will wonder, no doubt, why I discouraged the union between you and Zain. I'm ashamed to admit that the real reason for my disapproval was that I did not think Zain could survive without me. It's nothing Oedipal, I assure you. I just thought he was too fragile to withstand a relationship, especially with someone as strong as you. I now recognize the folly of my ways.

The more you two thrived as a couple—I heard about your relationship from your Uncle Anil incessantly—the more I convinced myself that it would not last. I dug myself deeper and deeper into a crevasse that I couldn't escape. What mother wants to believe that another woman can take care of her baby? Especially a baby who is so delicate, even well into adulthood.

If you become a mother, you will understand why I acted as I did. I would love to be a grandmother, and any child would be lucky to have you two as parents. My Zain's vulnerability would make him an excellent father. He is so protective of those he loves. I am not taking a stance on whether you should embark on parenthood, or even if you should get married. I only want to say that you have my blessing, whatever you choose. And I promise you that I will always be here for you, regardless of what happens between you and Zain.

I've said enough—too much, in fact—but it needed to be documented. If not for posterity's sake, then for yours, precious Aliseeya. For you are as dear to me as my own child—my one and only, beloved Prince Zain.

Affectionately yours,
Auntie Gulnar.

Chapter 39

Nairobi, 2011

Owing to a technical issue with the aircraft he was meant to take from Nairobi to Dar es Salaam, Zain was forced to spend a night in the Kenyan capital. The airline provided him with a complimentary hotel room. Although it was near to the airport, its setting was not what one might describe as pleasing—the smell of cow manure pervaded.

The hotel possessed a faded old-world glory. It appeared an establishment whose managers believed they could conceal all manner of sins behind velvet curtains. A cursory drawing of the curtains by Zain, revealing a dusty windowsill, quickly put paid to that theory.

Zain could see the missed calls on his mobile. Aliseeya had been trying to reach him all evening. He finally answered a call from her well after midnight, UK time. Aliseeya expressed both delight and surprise at reaching him.

"What're you doing up so late, Zain?"

"Speaking to you."

"Ha-ha. Obvs. I meant, apart from that, Mister Clever Chops."

"Attempting to find hot water with which to bathe."

"So then it's true—Dar is as infrastructurally challenged as everyone says it is?"

"Nairobi, actually. I'm not in Dar yet. My connecting flight was grounded here."

"In that case, you should be sweet! Nairobi's quite modern, as Africa goes. I stayed at the Stanley, and it was charming."

"I'm sure Nairobi proper is charming, Ali, but they've put me up in some God-forsaken hovel surrounded by cattle fields."

"Ah yes, the anywhere-in-Africa look. I've seen it in many countries. Tell me one thing: what fabric are the curtains made of?"

"Velvet."

"Say no more. You poor man! If my previous experience is anything to go by, you're not having a hot shower tonight. You should check if there is a kettle in your room. If so, you can pour some boiled water into the bath."

"Ta. That's a nice suggestion. Anyway, how are you holding up? It's late for you, isn't it?"

"Not as late as it is for you, Z."

"Listen babe, this is costing me a small fortune. Shall we try to Skype tomorrow? Of course, it means we'll have to place our faith in Tanzanian Wi-Fi."

"Um…yes, babe. Let's try to connect earlier tomorrow. Okay, Zain? I'd like to know that you've reached Dar safely. And of course, any news of your mum as soon as you can, yeah?"

"Naturally, darling."

"First, *babe*. And now, *darling*? Is something wrong?"

"Hey, I can call you darling if I want! Nothing is wrong. Far from it. I feel great! Notwithstanding the late hour, the cow paddies, the cold water, the dust, the—"

"Blimey! It sounds like a great time, indeed!"

They both laughed.

"Seriously, I'm glad to have made it to Africa. I'm not happy that it's in pursuit of my mad mother, but hey-ho."

"It's good you're there."

"I know. But please don't tell Mum about this. That is, if we all start speaking again."

"I won't. Good night, Zain."

"Good night, Aliseeya darling."

Chapter 40

Aliseeya Justice came from good people. Damaris Justice, for one, had worked hard to live up to the exalted surname she had adopted from her late husband, Orlando. Her efforts to act justly would have pleased her parents. Born in Kingston, Jamaica, to Clarice and Martin Dixon, Damaris was raised to be gracious in everything she did. Throughout her childhood, her mother, Clarice, had chanted her favorite maxim to Damaris: "However many times you give thanks, it is not enough."

So I'm supposed to be thankful that my husband died on me after only twelve years of marriage? I should give thanks that I must now raise my baby girl, Aliseeya, on my own? Tell me, Lord, is that justice?

At the time of Orlando's untimely passing, Clarice had rung from Jamaica to comfort her.

"Chile, at least you got twelve years wid' him."

"Twelve years not enough, Mudda. I got a pickney to raise on me own."

"Aliseeya, baby? She'll be fine, chile. Aliseeya is strong-strong. You hear what me say?"

"I know, I know. Me ah strong-strong, too."

"Exactly, my girl. You got to praise the Lord for what husband he gave you. Never mind for how long."

"It doesn't seem just that he was taken, but I'm going to be a proper Justice woman all the same."

"Yes, pickney! That's the spirit. Lord knows your Orlando Justice, he was a mighty good man, that one. Bless up!"

Damaris remembered it like it was only yesterday, not the twenty-plus years it had been.

Like a fool, I still miss that man.

She could never forget the look on his face when he had eaten that blasted poisoned cod in Swansea. *Why fish and chips, for heaven's sake? I hate that stuff. I would rather nyam some roti and curry goat any day of the week.*

Against her protestations, Orlando had insisted on ordering fish and chips for himself.

"We must try to live a little—not too much, mind you—like these English people do."

Orlando Justice had missed the irony of his making such a declaration while the family was on a camping holiday in Wales. Or the fact that fish and chips was not an indigenous English dish. It had been brought over by Jewish migrants. Since he had immigrated to Britain, Orlando had been fixated on adopting English ways. He was the opposite of his friend Anil Jaffar, who favored African politics, Persian poetry, and Indian food. Orlando would tell Anil that he was culturally confused.

"No, no, not for me, man, all this mick-and-picks."

Anil was too kind to tell his friend that the word he was looking for was pick-and-mix.

"But Orlando, English culture as we understand it today, is itself a pick-and—I mean, a mélange. Tea drinking originated in China, the Queen's crown jewels were taken from India, and the numerals we use are Arabic."

"Mélange? Nice one, using a French word to illustrate your point. All right man! I give you that. One for Team Jaffar."

There were never any hard feelings between Orlando and Anil. The two would spend hours in Anil's upstairs study, listening to Harry Belafonte records, sharing stories from Jamaica and Tanzania, and laughing so loudly that Gulnar would sometimes climb the stairs and shush them.

"Quiet please, you two rascals!" She would be smiling as she said this, clearly reveling in her husband's bonhomie with his mate. "Don't you know that Aliseeya and Zain are napping?"

"Sorry, Gulnar. It won't happen again," Orlando said, over the sound of Anil sniggering.

"Thanks, Orlando. Say, why don't you ring Damaris at the hospital and ask her to come round for dinner after her shift ends? You and Aliseeya are already here, and it would be nice for the children to spend more time together. You know what a fuss they make when it's time for them to leave each other."

"Tell me about it! Every Friday night, Aliseeya be asking, *Am I going to see Zain this weekend?*"

"God bless them, the little angels," said Anil.

"Little devils, more like. Anyway, what do you say, Orlando? Will you ring Damaris and have dinner with us?"

"Cheers, Gulnar. That would be splendid! Come to think of it, we should all go out for one of those, what they be calling it? Donut kebabs?"

"Doner kebabs," Anil said gently.

Orlando never felt defensive when Anil helped him with a word.

"That's a lovely idea, Orlando."

"Thanks, Gulnar."

"In fact, there is a new kebab shop in the high street, just next to Streatham Common station. I pass it every day on my way to work. The only problem is, what do we do with the children?"

She was referring to the experience of dining out in Britain in the 1980s. In those days, restaurants, and especially cafés of the sort which the Justices and Jaffars could afford, were filled with adults who had swilled plenty of lagers and spirits in the local pub, smoking like chimneys. Anil was virulently anti-smoking,

"I think you're right, Gully. We can't take the kids to that place. Orlando and I will walk over to the high street, pick up some kebabs and chips, and bring them back here. We can all eat in the garden if the weather remains dry."

"Dry? The place looks like a Borneo jungle, Anil."

"Is that your subtle way of reminding me that I haven't done the weeding?"

"Was I being subtle? I didn't mean to be."

Sensing the tension, Orlando jumped in.

"Hee-hee, good one, Gully! Borneo. Ha-ha! Listen though, I agree with Anil. We will sort out the food, so long as you don't mind staying here with the pickneys while we buy the food. I'll go and ring Damaris to see if the plan suits her. If I could just use your hall phone?"

"Yes, of course, Orlando. You are at home here."

As soon as Orlando was out of earshot, Gulnar told her husband, "And listen, mister. Don't buy too many chips!"

Anil had a reputation for bringing back double the quantity of whatever he was tasked with purchasing. He and Gulnar had a dance about shopping that went back and forth. But however precise her instructions, they were no use. He always bought too much. She tried reducing the quantities she requested.

"Please bring back only one tomato from the corner shop, Anil."

Knowing he doubled everything, she expected him to come home with two tomatoes. Anil would instinctively judge the request as a miscalculation by Gulnar. He assumed that any recipe would call for at least two tomatoes, so he doubled that number, proudly entering the house with four tomatoes.

Damaris also had her share of annoyances from her husband. Mainly that Orlando did not like to eat home-cooked food, especially Caribbean dishes. Gulnar would come to the rescue, inviting the Justices 'round for dinner so that Orlando could feel that he was eating out, without busting the family's budget.

Orlando, like Anil, often came home with grocery items that his wife was not pleased to encounter. One time, it was a frozen blue and white box. Damaris was livid. "Orlando, what have you gone and brought, man?"

"Quiet yourself, woman! These are fish fingers."

"Tell me one ting—how fish can have fingers? Do they have hands?"

"What are you going on about? These are all the rage. All the other fellows' wives make them for their husbands."

"Why you gotta go and buy all this foolishness when we have Brixton Market just down the road? I can go and get some nice hacki, plantain—"

"Nah, man."

"Well, what am I supposed to do with these silly tings? You think Aliseeya is going to eat something called fingers?"

"That girl will eat what is given to her. She already getting too uppity."

"I am going to telephone Gulnar. She'll know what to do with these tings." Damaris walked to her front parlor, kissing her teeth.

"Don't you be making them sounds at me, woman! I'm only trying to liven things up a bit, you know. Ain't no harm in that."

"I'm sick of your livening things up with chupid food! One day, all your foolishness is gonna catch up with you. You hear what me say?"

"Damaris, my sweet coconut woman. Calm yourself."

"What you be calling me that for? You been listening to too much Harry Belafonte with Anil." But she was smiling.

God, I miss that coconut man! Does that make me a coconut widow? Now, if our Aliseeya baby could just get on with it already and marry Zain!

On that fateful night in Swansea, Damaris's cutting words to Orlando came back to haunt her. *One day, all your foolishness is gonna catch up with you.*

There was nothing especially foolish about ordering cod and chips at a local caff in Swansea. How was Orlando to know that his piece of fish contained mercury?

Damaris deeply regretted reprimanding her husband about the fish fingers on that day. Of course, nothing she could have said, or not said, would have changed Orlando's predilection for eating out, and for trying strange English foods, like black pudding.

My poor Orlando. It's not his fault he was so obsessed with English-ness. I just wish I could have saved him from that blasted fish.

Orlando had been so obstinate about eating out that her feeling of being irked remained with her long after he was gone. Since his death, Damaris had been equally stubborn, refusing to eat anything not prepared by her own hands, including every loaf of bread.

Aliseeya went to the other extreme, scouring the planet's most turbulent places just to take pictures, and eating everything from mopane worms in Botswana to scorpions in Thailand.

She had told Damaris about Zain's trip to Tanzania in search of Gulnar. *How long will it be before Aliseeya follows that boy? My baby girl, she's gonna follow Zain wherever he goes. A mother's lot is to worry. Oh Lord, tell me, when will it stop?*

***

Gulnar, too, was plagued by maternal worries.

I hope Zainul conveyed my message properly. What if this is too much for Zain? I don't want him to hate me even more. Being his mother has been the hardest struggle of my life. I pray that one day, he appreciates all I've done for him. In the meantime, here I am in beautiful Dar es Salaam. What more could I ask for?

Chapter 41

Dar es Salaam, 2011

It is said of some bureaucracies that the only efficiency one can rely on them for is that they will conduct business in the most inefficient manner possible. The next day, despite the unfavorable weather conditions, air traffic congestion, and what one airline official told Zain was "a lack of permission to fly," he finally made it to Dar es Salaam. The case of his hour-and-a-half flight from Nairobi to Dar taking the better part of twelve hours proved this maxim about bureaucracies.

Zain was so exhausted that he checked into his hotel, ordered a simple chicken curry from room service, ate it, and went to sleep. Although it was his first time traveling outside of Europe, and he was generally anxious about being in new environments, Zain was not worried about his stomach, as he had been raised on Gulnar's and Damaris's chicken curries.

***

Given the stormy weather passing over the East African coast, Gulnar found herself confined to her hotel. She wandered around the hotel lobby, browsing shops clearly designed for travelers who would not venture far beyond tourist traps. She thought it sad that people would come all the way to Tanzania and then limit themselves to these few oceanside enclaves. What about the heady heights of Lushoto, with its majestic cliffs looking down onto a verdant sea of foliage? Or Iringa, with its stolid, stony hills, and its proximity to the vast, ethereal Ruaha National Park?

Who comes to Dar just to buy trinkets in hotel shops? Not me. I have a purpose. Even for those without a connection to this place, Tanzania is rich with culture, history, and natural beauty, despite the best efforts of the British and the Germans to bleed it dry. In the end, Africa will outlast all violence wrought upon it. As in Ogbuefi Ezeugo's speech in the copy of Things Fall Apart, gifted to me by Aliseeya: Those sons of wild animals have dared to murder a daughter of Umuofia.

Tears streamed down Gulnar's face as she sat reading in the hotel lobby. *Mungu ibariki Afrika.*

Chapter 42

A liseeya finally got hold of her busy mother, who had been working extra shifts at the hospital to cover for the parents who were squeezing out the last of their annual leave for the summer, before their children returned to school. Damaris knew something was wrong the minute she heard her daughter's voice.

"Hi, Mum. Where've you been?"

"Mostly working, my darling. Are you all right, pickney?"

"Yes, of course. Why shouldn't I be?"

"It's normally me chasing you down on the telephone, not the other way around."

"Well, if I'm honest, there's something the matter with Zain."

"Oh no! I pity that poor boy, having to run after Gulnar wid' all of her foolishness in Africa." Damaris kissed her teeth.

"No, it's not that."

"What is it, love? Is he feeling okay? I hope he took anti-malarial tablets with him."

"His physical health is fine, Mum."

"Then what could it be? Come out with it, child."

"I ran into Malcolm, Zain's boss, the other day, while grocery shopping at Tesco. We know each other because we work in different parts of the same building."

"Yes, and so what? What kind of Malcolm story is this?"

"When he asked me about Zain, I said he's with his family. I left out the bit about him chasing down his mum—who has clearly gone bonkers—in Tanzania."

"You did the right thing, love. Bosses can be so judgmental. I remember after your papa died, I wanted to go to church—on a Sunday, no less—and they wouldn't give me the time off. Stupid jobsworths!"

"Oh gosh, I didn't know that, Mum! That must have been hard on you."

"'Twas. But we ain't getting anywhere with your story, baby girl. Now, tell mama what's the matter."

"The newspaper is going to let go of Zain."

"No! Oh no! No, no, no! The poor love. As if he hasn't got enough to deal with already. What, with him losing his daddy, chasing after that madwoman Gulnar…and now this. Oh, the shame of it." She produced another kiss of the teeth. "Life just ain't been fair to that boy."

"I know."

After a pause, Damaris said, "I've just had an idea, Ali baby. Listen closely."

"I'm all ears, Mum."

"I'm telling you this because I love that Zain like he was my own child. You know that. And I see what goes on in the hospital, and the psychiatric ward. You tell that sweet boy to go to take his dismissal case to employment tribunal, with a claim of discrimination."

"What? I can't believe you just said that, Mum!"

"Don't *mum* me, chile. We both know he ain't right in the head, the poor dear. Lord bless him. What his mum is doing now only proves it runs in the family, don't it?"

"You're saying he has a disability?"

"I'm positive he does. You listen to me now, Miss Aliseeya Justice. That Zain, he has always been different. I used to watch him as a little lad. He played with you fine and good 'cause he trusted you. If any other child came down the road, he'd go running into the house. I'm telling you, he ain't right in the head."

"Do you think it's an anxiety disorder?"

"I can't say exactly what's wrong with him, now can I? I'm a nurse, not a doctor. But it's something, I'm sure of it."

"Blimey! I'm kind of shocked. But not altogether surprised, if that makes sense."

"It does, dear. It will be a shock for you. I understand. But it need not change anything between you two, you hear what me say?"

"Well, I guess—"

"No time for guessing, my girl. That Zain of yours is a good man, Aliseeya, and you're going to stand by him, you hear? He loves you something fierce."

"I know. Of course you're right, Mum. Look, I'm going to need time to absorb what you're saying about Zain. In the meantime, the problem of his being dismissed from his job still remains."

"No problem. When he comes back from Tanzania, we take him to see a doctor. They diagnose him. The hard part would be getting him to see the doctor in the first place, though. Men don't like doctors, and they can be stubborn as old goats. Just look at your father and his insistence on eating fish and chips." Damaris kissed her teeth.

"Really, Mum? You must stop torturing yourself with the refrain, *Your daddy, he ate poisoned fish. Your daddy, he ate poisoned fish.* Enough already. Lord have mercy! You know, I miss Papa, too. But by not letting go, you're the one being stubborn."

"Well..." Damaris sighed, "that told me, didn't it?"

"Look, I don't want to get into a scrap, Mother. Can we get back to the problem at hand? My boyfriend—who I've just discovered might be unwell—is about to be sacked."

"Okay, okay. It seems to me all you have to do is somehow prove that one of his bosses—it could be anyone at the paper, not just Malcom—knows about Zain's condition."

"That's just it. From what Malcolm said, I think they're closing his entire department. Zain is not being fired, per se. It's a redundancy based on restructuring. Malcolm was trying to be kind by giving me a heads-up. I think he has a soft spot for Zain. It will be very difficult to prove that it was a case of unfair dismissal or discrimination."

"Ah, I got you now. Hmmm. Look, darlin', I've got to go. My oven timer just went off. I'm making a tangerine cake for my colleague's leaving do at the hospital. Can I call you later?"

"Sure, Mum. Thanks for being there. Sorry about earlier. I really do miss Papa, but I don't think it will make us feel better to go on about the poisoned fish."

"Dat's all right. You don't got to thank me. That's my job. Do you hear what me say? And about the scrap—it's okay. I know you'll be defending your father until your dying day. You're a Justice woman, through and through."

"That, I am. All right, Mum. Enough of the soppy stuff. Cheerio. Love ya."

"Now I know you be worried!" Damaris laughed. "You never tell me you love me! Love you too, baby girl."

"Cheers."

"Toodle-oo, darling."

Chapter 43

So far, I'm not loving Dar.

After two full days of bed rest, Zain was starting to feel better. He was now able to stand up—a marked improvement over the previous forty-eight hours. His round-the-clock visits to the toilet were also drawing down in frequency. The curry chicken he had ordered from room service had not been so innocuous after all.

Zain knew he should inform the hotel of his condition so that no other guests would face the risk of being poisoned by the ghastly curry. But as always, he hesitated about how exactly to approach them. He felt that walking up to the reception desk with this news would be too aggressive. Conversely, calling them on the phone would be too passive. He was stuck in a trap of his mind's own making. If only Aliseeya were here, she'd know how to take care of it.

> *Stop it. Stop being a baby and wanting to rely on her for everything. You're a grown man, Zain Jaffar.*

And why hadn't he heard from her since his arrival? If the situation were reversed, and he'd gone into radio silence for two days, he would never hear the end of it. *Women.* That thought reminded him of why he was in this God-forsaken town in the first place. *I've got to track down that doolally mother of mine. God help me.*

Steeling himself for more contact with new people who spoke an unknown language, in this strange, searing-hot city, Zain showered, dressed, and walked down to the lobby, studiously avoiding the front desk and any mention of that vicious chicken curry. After procuring a taxi with the help of the concierge, Zain asked the driver to take him to Upanga, the neighborhood of his mother's youth.

How can Dar es Salaam be the abode of peace? Where his mother had perceived beautiful trees and lawns, Zain saw fetid palm fronds hanging off the swaying branches, and burnt-out patches of grass which spelt depression. The flowers and fruits, of which Gulnar had gushed in her missives, were surrounded by nasty insects buzzing away. The bougainvillea-lined avenues about which she had reminisced—some leading directly to the sparkling Indian Ocean—Zain regarded as bumpy deathtraps powdered with dust, giving off a heat so visceral that it seemed to hover just above the asphalt.

Everywhere he looked, he found Tanzanians straining to survive under the scorching sun. The gleaming white buildings about which Gulnar had waxed nostalgic, appeared to Zain as though they needed a paint job. For the life of him, he could not see what his mother had loved about this place.

The taxi driver managed to locate the Aga Khan Mzizima School, the only landmark Zain could think of in relation to his mother. He remained in the back seat of the parked car as he battled his thoughts. He was afraid to go inside the school, or to talk to anyone. What would he say to them? He couldn't just rock up and say, *"Hello, my name is Zain Jaffar. Have you seen my mother, the former Miss Gulnar Kassam? She was head teacher of this school forty years ago. By the way, she has lost all her marbles and run away from her London home, which is why I am here."*

Even entertaining such a conversation was absurd. They would be sure to think *he* was the one who was a few cards short of a full deck.

That's the last thing I need in this God-forsaken place.

***

Gulnar, meanwhile, was starting to wonder if Zain would ever appear. A quick phone call to her friend Zainul in Northampton confirmed that she had relayed the message on Gulnar's behalf. Zainul called Zain a cheeky boy, but Gulnar dismissed this.

My Zain has always been gentle as a rose. He might become defensive when cornered, but he has never spoken a harsh word to anyone. I know I'm not blameless. I have cornered him into this situation where he has to find me. It's probably stressing him out, bicharo. However, I had no choice. It was my last and only option, and I did it for his own good.

Chapter 44

A day after yet another tangerine cake went down a treat at her colleague's leaving do, Damaris Justice finally worked up the courage to ring Aliseeya.

"Aliseeya, baby?"

"Hi, Mum."

"How you doing? Not too cold up there in Scotland, I hope?"

"Not at all. Mum, I know you're stalling, asking me about the weather."

"Well, there is no easy way to say this to you, pickney."

"I'm listening."

"If you want Zain to survive this redundancy with some shred of dignity left in him, you got to get ahead of him."

"I don't follow."

"You tell him you got a job offer in London that you can't refuse, and you're both moving back here. End of story."

"Okaaaay. You know I'd move back in a heartbeat, but is it really that simple? I mean, I know we only came up here in the first place because of Auntie Gulnar—"

"Yah, I know all dat. But now you got to sort this out while Zain is away. Double fast. You hear what me say? Present it to him like it's all been planned, and like your job opportunity is too good to pass up. I'm sure you can get something with the presswire agency. They loved you."

"Yes, I think I could wrangle a job with the agency. My photos of the London riots have done well, which has helped my profile."

"You mean all dem fool boys stealing trainers from the high street shops?" Damaris kissed her teeth.

"Look, Mum, I just cover the news. I don't make it. Besides, at least people now know who Mark Duggan was."

"It's a shame about that poor boy."

"It really is. But let's get back to my boy, and what we're going to do to help him."

"Just come back to London, baby. Dat's your solution. You hear what me say?"

"I do. I mean, I have kept in touch with some agency colleagues, including my old manager. But even if I could make all of that happen in a jiffy, Zain would still receive an official redundancy notice from Malcolm."

"This is the ingenious part of my plan. Your mother's been thinking hard while baking tangerine cake, you know."

"I'm all ears."

"You use your connection with this Malcolm to ask him not to say anything to Zain. Let Zain think *he's the one* resigning. I'm sure his boss won't mind. Especially because of your ace card."

"And what might that ace card be?"

"You imply that Zain would have a case against the paper. How you do that is up to you. I know you could twist anyone round your little finger. You always have been charming, since you were a little girl."

"Hmmm. I'm not sure, Mum. That is very devious. It's basically blackmail. *Let Zain resign, or he'll take you to court.*"

"Not at all, child. That's the way of the world. I see it every day at the hospital. You got to be one step ahead of them just to survive."

"But how do I convince Malcolm that Zain would have a case?"

"That's the beauty of it. You don't have to. You point out—subtly—that the onus would be on his employers to prove that they didn't know about his condition. Zain's work has always been outstanding, no?"

"Well, yes. He writes well enough, even if he's not good with people. They mainly assign him stories that don't require interviews, but he's still one of the best journalists on staff."

"There you are. And his bosses are not going to want this coming out in the news. They're a newspaper themselves, for God's sake. Employment tribunals are public, and they can get ugly."

"Not too ugly, I hope. Remember, I work for the same organization."

"Never mind all that, chile. Just leave Glasgow already."

"I'd love to, but—"

"No *buts*. You hear what me say? The threat of going public with this should be enough. Lord have mercy, you should see the list of cases against the National Health Service. It makes us look so bad! Even if Zain's bosses were to win the case, the damage to their reputation would raggedy."

"Wow, you really have thought this one through."

"Yes." Damaris was smiling, happy that she would have her baby back home in London.

But the thought of the deception she was suggesting wiped the smile off her face.

"Mum, you still there?"

"Yes, yes. Sorry, I got lost in my happy thoughts of you returning to London."

"I don't know if I can do this, Mum."

Damaris kissed her teeth. "Now you listen to meet good and proper, Miss Aliseeya Justice. You *got* to do this. You don't have a choice. That lovely Zain, he can't take no more after all that he's been through. Otherwise, I fear he'll go down the road his mother is racing away on at breakneck speed."

"I know," Aliseeya whispered.

"And you owe it to him. Well, not owe, exactly. But if there is something you can do to help someone you love, then I believe you ought to do it. That's what my mother taught me."

"Awww. I miss Grandma Clarice."

"So do I, baby girl. So do I. You got to love Zain fiercely, the way Grandma Clarice loved us, remember?"

"Yup."

"After all, we've known the Jaffar family a long time. Almost your whole life, pickney. We keep them together, we keep ourselves together. Do you hear what me say?"

"Sure."

"Your Uncle Anil, he treated your papa just like a brother. God rest their souls. Oh, chile, those two used to laugh like schoolboys. And that family, they've always been good to us. Well, except that chupid Gulnar these last few years. Lord, I used to love that woman like my own sister, too." With a sigh, Damaris kissed her teeth again.

"Mother, you're getting sidetracked."

"Yes, I know. So anyway, as I was saying. Sometimes you got to take care of someone in a way that they can't do for themselves. And it would be nice, baby. Just think about it. I'm not going to lie. I'd be happy to have you back home. And it would be good for Zain and his foolish mother, too, whatever she is up to right now in Dar es Salaam."

"Yep."

"That's all you got to say?"

"Okay, you're right."

"Now I know me lovely daughter is fresh out of choices! You never chat to me like *mother knows best*."

"Seriously, Mum, what you've suggested is a wicked, ingenious plan. I need to get right onto my contacts in London. And I'll have to arrange to see Malcolm again, in person. I can't put any of this in writing, you understand."

"You run along, child. You're my brave, talented girl. Do you hear what me say? No one is going to mess with you."

"Cheers, Mum. Bye."

"Toodle-oo, love."

Chapter 45

After driving around steamy Upanga all afternoon, Zain was at his wit's end. He needed something to settle his stomach, but didn't want to return to his hotel just yet.

I've got to find that woman. She could be in danger. I wonder if other sons go through such agony over their wayward mothers?

Upon spotting a little *duka* on the United Nations Road, Zain asked the driver to stop so that he could pick up a drink. A cold Fanta would hydrate him and provide a much-needed jolt of energy. After delivering a glass bottle of the fizzy orange liquid to his driver, Zain stood under the shade of the *duka's* awning and guzzled his soda.

Hearing the Muslim call to prayer in the distance, he was struck by an idea. He could go to the mosque. Even though he was not a regular attendee, he knew it was a tightknit community. Someone was bound to know Gulnar.

While asking the driver to take him straight there, Zain could feel his heart pulsing. *What is this? I have no reason to be nervous. Breathe.*

Upon arriving at the mosque, he hurried into the serene white building and removed his shoes. *This is it. She'd better be here.*

After washing the heat and dust from his face and hands, he steeled himself and entered the main hall. *I have no idea what to do. I guess I'll have to fake it.*

Immediately following prayers, just as Zain expected, he was approached by a kind-faced man.

"*As-salamu alaykum.* New to Dar es Salaam?"

"*Wa alaykumu as-salam.* Yes I am." *This is my worst nightmare.*

"Welcome, beta. From where?"

"London."

"Very good. Do you have a place to stay?"

There it was—the community hospitality his parents had talked about.

"I do."

"Son of?"

Here we go. "Anil Jaffar." Zain could see the man's face light up.

"Oh yes. He was from Dar es Salaam, no? Lovely man he was. An accountant, I think?"

"Yes."

The verifying of professions was a key element of the conversational dance with which Zain was familiar.

"I am very sorry for the loss of your father, my son. *Inna lillahi, wa inna ilayhi rajiun.* We all come from God, and to him we return."

News travels fast. "Thanks."

"You don't say much, do you, boy?"

"No." *Crazy mother, crazy mother. How do I mention my crazy mother?*

"So what brings you to Dar? Tracing your father's roots, isn't it?"

"No, not exactly." *Wait, this could be an in.* "Well, um, actually…in a way, yes. My mother is currently here studying her family history, and I've come to join her."

"Oh, very good, very good, son. We all need to learn about where we came from. Come, let us go out so I can introduce you to my wife. I am Brother Malik, by the way. Malik Sultan."

"Nice to meet you, Uncle Malik."

Zain understood this part of the niceties. After meeting a man, his wife would welcome the newcomer by issuing invitations.

"And you are?"

"I am Brother Zain. Jaffar, as you know."

"Very well. Come, Zain. That's a good boy." Malik gently placed his hand behind Zain's back as they walked out to the courtyard.

Why is he treating me like a child?

Malik spotted his wife and beckoned her over. Zain noticed that he did not address her by name.

"Come and meet this nice boy from London. He is the son of Anil Jaffar."

"*As-salamu alaykum*, beta. Welcome."

"*Salam.*" Zain noticed that she did not give her name. *Don't women have names in this country?*

"What is your name, Auntie?"

"Her name is Khadija," Malik interjected, as if intercepting a dangerous question.

And why can't they speak for themselves?

Khadija quickly added, "You may call me Auntie Sultan. Everybody does. All the young people in the mosque, that is. You must come over for dinner while you are here. What is your good name?"

"Zain."

"Come home sometime, okay, Zain? Arrange it with Uncle. Excuse me, I have to help with the cleaning. It was nice meeting you."

"Um, um, please wait one second, Auntie Sultan. I have a question."

Malik was looking at him quizzically.

"Yes, beta? What is it?"

It's now or never. "You see, I want to surprise my mum. She is here in Dar now, and doesn't yet know that I am here."

"Oh, *shabash.* Very good, son."

Why are you talking to me like I'm five years old? Or am I just delusional from the sickness?

"Thanks. You might know her. She used to be head teacher at the Aga Khan School. Her name before marriage was Gulnar Kassam."

"Oho! Yes, yes, of course, beta. Miss Kassam. Everybody in Dar es Salaam knows her. She was famous." Khadija let out a giggle, covering her mouth with her hand in embarrassment.

"Was she indeed?" *Please be so kind as to spare me your praise for Miss Tanzania.*

"Oh yes, very much so. Your mummy used to model in fashion shows, attend fancy parties, and hang around with big shots. You know, government people and such types." Khadjia was pointing upwards as she spoke, the implication being that *such types* were above her station, yet not on the right level spiritually.

"Um, how fascinating." *How do I get past this glorification stage?* Zain had heard glowing reports about Gulnar for years, and was uninterested.

"Given what you say about the parties she used to attend, where would be a nice place to take her out for dinner? I mean, where in Dar do you think she would most like to go?"

"Oh, Zain beta, that is too easy. Only one place you must take her: Oyster Bay Hotel."

God in heaven, that's it! That's where she's got to be.

"Thank you, Auntie Sultan."

"You are welcome, beta. God bless you."

Upon reaching Oyster Bay, Zain asked his driver to let him out, park the car, and wait, promising an extra tip. He had already paid for a full day's wages, but wanted the assurance of a ride back to his hotel. *Who knows what I'm in for.*

Opposite the front entrance of The Oyster Bay Hotel, Zain noticed a prominent walkway leading directly to the beach. This was the first beautiful sight he had encountered in dusty Dar es Salaam. The pavement was smooth and spotless. The hedges had been elegantly trimmed. There was no rubbish in sight, and the delicate scent of jasmine flowers pervaded.

At last, Zain could understand why the city had been named *Abode of Peace*. He was still furious with Gulnar for instigating his journey there, but beauty of the place was undeniable.

Just breathe, Zain, and remember Bob Marley's sage words: Don't worry about a thing, 'cause every little thing is gonna be all right.

Just as Marley sang about the peace evoked by Jamaica's beauty, the exquisiteness of the scene before Zain—azure sky, turquoise sea, pink flowers—induced a tranquility in him that he had never known.

Okay, so Mum was right about Tanzania. I'll still never tell her. Ugh, I feel sick. Breathe, Zain, breathe. He patted his turbulent stomach, hoping to calm it.

Blimey! Speak of the devil. Looking down to the far end of the walkway, he saw the silhouette of none other than his formidable mother, sashaying as if on a runway, pushing along what appeared to be a pram.

At first, Zain held back. His heart was pounding. He felt queasy, and he was unsure how to approach her. *If I startle her, she might run like a wild gazelle.*

After a moment's hesitation, he decided that he would sprint and surprise her before she could get away. *She can't outrun me, especially with a pram. It's truly now or never.*

Zain remembered how far he had traveled just to make sure that she was okay. He was at the end of his line.

As Zain raced toward his mother, he noticed that the pram she was pushing contained a baby doll wrapped in a blue kanga cloth.

He felt dizzy.

Suddenly noticing her son's rapid approach, Gulnar jolted awake as if from a trance.

"Zain! Oh, Zainy, my darling! You've come. Thank God."

As she reached out to embrace him, Zain was struck by a wash of pain. He doubled over, vomiting all over her Ferragamo flats.

Chapter 46

My Darling Zain,

This is my last letter. After this, we will resume life as normal and carry on as though nothing happened.

First, I must share one final story from Tanzania. During my recent stay at The Oyster Bay Hotel, I happened upon a lovely older woman taking afternoon tea. Seeing me walking past in my trademark white blouse and yellow skirt, she called out, "Are you Gulnar Kassam? Kulsum and Abdullah's daughter?"

"Yes, I am, Auntie."

After beckoning me to sit down, she recounted this story to me over oolong tea and kokotende. It was a tale about my father's mother that even my sister Roshan Ara, our oldest living relative, has never told me. This auntie at The Oyster Bay Hotel began by using a Swahili expression which is meant to evoke compassion, but may sound harsh in English.

"Your granny was a little soft in the head. That is what they used to say about her. But she was also gentle as a rose."

Apparently, my grandmother said little and kept to herself. She produced three boys, but left the raising of them to her husband.

On the rare occasions when she would deign to speak to my grandfather, she would shout out, "Eh, Kassam, listen well. I am going to see my mother."

"Oho, wife, you are failing to fulfill your obligations here!"

"There are people besides you to tell me what my obligations should be."

"Who exactly might these others be?"

"They are in here." She would grin and point her bony index finger to her head. "I am going to see my mother."

Her mother—my great grandmother—lived on the other side of Dar es Salaam's Kizinga River.

Seeing his wife's disconcerting display, my grandfather would take their three sons into a protective embrace and proclaim, "Very well. Be off with you, mad woman!"

Granny would repeat, "I am going to see my mother."

"You've already said that."

"I am going to see my mother."

She would repeat this mantra as she walked along the dusty lanes of Kariakoo, making her way to the other side of the Kizinga River. After she returned home from these visits to her mother, it would be as though no discord had ever occurred. Neither Granddad nor Granny would refer to their earlier arguments.

Granny would cook dinner for the boys and tuck them into bed with stories of their maternal grandmother, whom they were never allowed to see. The boys—Gulamhusein, Janmohamed, and Abdullah—lived for these stories. They would gobble up their mother's colorful descriptions like sweets, which she recited under the cover of darkness.

One day, the usual exchange between Granny and Granddad took place. She added, "You do not understand me," to her refrain.

Walking along the dusty Karikoo streets, Granny muttered, "I am going to see my mother. You do not understand me."

Oblivious to everyone's stares, she continued walking and chanting, "I am going to see my mother. You do not understand me."

The people in the streets of Karikoo recognized Mrs. Kassam and knew better than to engage with her, seeing her as a large, exotic bird with a hint of menace—an ostrich, perhaps—who should not be toyed with.

That night, she did not return. Furious at her waywardness, Granddad asked his own mother—my other great-grandmother—to come 'round, feed the boys, and put them to bed.

The boys loved their grandmother. They ate and slept with content. None asked after their mother except for the youngest, my father, Abdullah.

The next morning, Granddad awoke to the commotion of fishermen at the door. They carried a huge, long sack into the house—wrapped in a white sheet—and placed it on the living room floor. The stench coming from the front of the house woke the boys—my father most of all. Holding his nose, Abdullah asked his father, Kassam, why they could not rid their house of this refuse.

Calmly, Granddad said, "That is your mother."

So you see, son—we descend from a family with a troubled history. My father's mother had a mental illness, but in those days, little was known or done about such conditions, apart from condemning those who suffered from them, making their lives worse.

No one can explain exactly how your great-grandmother died. The auntie at The Oyster Bay Hotel told me that it was not known whether Granny deliberately walked into the Indian Ocean, or whether she mistook it for the Kizinga River. Our role is not to judge, but to love. Which brings me to you, my lovely son.

I shall not mince my words, Zain. You have been diagnosed with borderline personality disorder. Your being weakened by food poisoning in Dar was a blessing in disguise. I was able to get you onto the next London flight and check you straight into St. George's Hospital. While you were there, Damaris asked a psychiatrist colleague of hers to see you. The two of you chatted extensively, though I suspect that remains a blur for you. It is thanks to your conversation with him that we now know what I have always suspected and feared.

When you were in school, the teachers told us you were gifted. They wanted to move you into a specialized program, and your father was ready to sign the papers to place you there. I did not want to separate you from your peers, so I stood my ground.

"I do not want Zainy to be separated from his age group. I don't want the labels *special* or *gifted* affixed to our boy."

"Why not?" your father asked.

"Because I don't want him to be treated differently, even if he is more intelligent. Nor do I want him to treat others differently, or think himself superior."

"Zain is not like that. He is kind to everyone."

"Nonetheless, separating him from children his age will only harm him. Trust me, Anil, I'm a teacher. Zainy is happy where he is. Let him remain there."

Your daddy and I argued about it for weeks. But in the end, he relented. You were not moved. You performed well in your A-levels, went on to study at St. Andrews University, and now you're a journalist. I'm so proud of you. I know you struggle to make friends, but once you get past the awkward stage, you're fine. Look at you and Aliseeya. You're as close as ever.

Even if you accept all that I have written, you may wonder why I went to Tanzania. It was for you, Zain. After your father's death, I wrote to you, I beseeched, I tried in every which way to connect with you. It was your daddy's dying wish that we should be reconciled. When my letters produced only silence on your part, I resolved to undertake an act so extreme that you would be forced to come to my rescue. I had faith that you would, for you still love me.

I acknowledge that it was an extreme plan. However, there is no denying that it has given you a new lease of life. It has released you from the hostility you harbored toward me for five years. Now you are free, and living here in London, where you belong. Your beloved Aliseeya Justice is also back home, just around the corner, so you two can be as close as you have been since your early days.

I know that living with me is not the same as having your own flat, but you need me, and I can take care of you. I hope you see that I only did all of this to evoke a loving response in you. I wanted you to understand that you should love a person, whatever their state of mind. I knew you would go to the ends of the earth to find me, and that your concern for me transcended all my transgressions.

The tables have turned. Do you see? I did not approve of your relationship with Aliseeya—wrongly, I admit—because I worried you would flounder. Yes, she loves you, but you did struggle. You need me, Zain. Just as you loved me when you thought I had lost my marbles, I want you to love yourself.

Now that we are reunited and living under the same roof, let us not speak of this anymore. I know your beloved father is smiling down on us, singing Harry Belafonte's *Coconut Woman,* with his dear friend, Orlando Justice. Let that be your guiding vision, Zain.

Oh, how Daddy loved you. Just pronouncing your name in your absence would bring tears to his eyes. You were always his precious angel, even when you were thirty-four years old, at his death. He could not live without you. Your first four years in Glasgow were the most painful period of his life. I say this to be truthful, not hurtful. Everything must come out now. Let there be no more deception in this family, my beloved son.

Your father's most important lesson for you—which must remain with you forever—is that you were brought into this world out of love. No one can harm you. No one can tell you that you are not normal. If they do, you must tell them that we are not here to judge each other. Remember that, my love. You originated from love, and you have returned to it.

Your loving mother,
Gulnar Jaffar (née Kassam)

Chapter 47

Zain's reaction to Gulnar's rescue mission to Dar es Salaam was unadulterated rage. For weeks after his return, Zain swam in a turbid stew of shock, resentment, and helplessness.

He missed his dad. Anil would never have supported Gulnar's conspiracy to entrap him. In that way, Zain's grief was purposive. He felt a new, acute sense of the loss of his father now that he really needed someone who understood him.

Zain barely spoke to Gulnar. He passed his days skulking around Streatham Common and walking the streets that had permeated his childhood. He would wordlessly acknowledge his mum at breakfast, taking his tea out to the garden when the weather permitted. Then he would leave the house all day, every day. He sometimes ran into the Somali shopkeepers who had known him since he was a boy, or, less frequently, former school friends emerging from Streatham Station. Mostly, he kept to himself. While wallowing in London's anonymity, he missed Glasgow.

Every evening, Zain would meet Aliseeya for dinner on Streatham High Road. On top of the oddness of living with their mothers, their relationship had moved from the relative bliss of sharing a Glaswegian flat, to this new separation. And while her career had taken off since their return to London, he was still too muddled to even think about work.

Finally, after a couple months of patiently waiting for him to snap out of it, Aliseeya had it out with Zain.

"So Zain, how long are you going to carry on feeling sorry for yourself?"

"I'm not feeling sorry for myself."

"No?"

"No. And that's flat."

"Then how would you describe this funk you're in?"

"I'm not in a funk."

"I see. If that's the case, then why don't you get off your duff and find a job?"

"Oi! Please, baby."

"Don't *baby* me!"

"Okay, sorry. Look, I'm still working through my..."

"Your what?"

"My anger."

"Aha!"

"What? Aha?"

"With whom are you angry?"

"I think you know the answer."

"Say it."

"My mum."

"So what?"

"So what? How could she have done this to me? By which I mean, concoct such an elaborate plot, fake her own senility, run away to Dar es Salaam, and pull me into her drama?"

"You tell me. Why did she do it?"

"You don't get to ask me anything, Ali."

"Why not?"

"Because you were in on it."

"I was not."

"You were, too. You took the opportunity of my traveling to Tanzania to become a co-conspirator."

"That's not how it went down."

"Oh yeah? How did it go down, then?"

"Things were happening quickly, and I..."

"You what? Asked Malcolm to make me redundant."

"No, Zain. How could you even think that?"

"I don't know precisely what your role was. All I remember is waking up in Saint George's Hospital, being informed that I was out of a job, and that we'd left Glasgow. You can imagine my surprise at finding out that my whole life had been turned upside down. It was bad enough that Gulnar should deceive me, but she was not the person who packed up the flat, moved our belongings down to London, handed me my P45, and said that it was *all for the best*. The whole time I was in Dar, I had an ominous feeling that you were plotting something."

"I guess I do owe you an explanation," Aliseeya said, "but you're not going to like it. While you were in Dar, I ran into Malcolm in the shops, and he told me your job was on the line. I went to great lengths to quickly find a job in London, plan our return, and spare you the humiliation of being sacked. It's just a coincidence that your mother...did what she did. You know I think she's crackers, too."

"Codswallop! You expect me to believe that pack of lies?"

"I swear it's true. You're just being para—"

"Cat got your tongue?"

"I'm not afraid to say it. You're being paranoid. Anyway, let's get down to brass tacks. I'd rather be frank. After all, I swore that I wasn't going to treat you any differently."

"Treat me differently?"

"You know. After all that has happened."

"You're being cryptic, Aliseeya. It doesn't suit you."

"Don't be such a plonker!"

"I'm not. I just want you to say whatever it is that you're dancing around."

"Hey, that's not right! I was trying to pull you out of your self-pity by having you acknowledge it. You've completely turned the conversation around."

"It's good to know I still have that cognitive ability."

"Zainy, your diagnosis doesn't have to change anything."

"Aha! Now we're getting down to the nitty-gritty. My diagnosis?"

"Not acknowledging it won't make it go away, babes."

"Just like you, I don't trust you when you *babes* me."

"Zain, you're being impossible. I can't go on watching you hurt yourself."

"I'm not hurting myself."

"All right, then who is hurting you?"

Aliseeya had trapped him. He couldn't very well mention Gulnar again. What grown man sits at dinner with his girlfriend, repeating, *"My mother is hurting me?"*

And she wasn't, really. She had infuriated him with her underhanded plot, but he had to admit that it had been for his own good. Though, he would never openly acknowledge this.

He was refusing to face the very thing that had eluded him his entire life. Now that it was right there—every morning when he woke up under his mother's roof, and every night when he retired under it—he just couldn't bear to acknowledge it. Might it just be easier to look it straight in the eye and move on with his life? The monster he had been grappling with for as long as he could remember had only been strengthened by his denials.

After a long silence, he came back. He saw the recognition in Aliseeya's eyes. She smiled even before he started to speak.

"Right. I'll start looking for work tomorrow."

"That's my Zain!"

"I'm back, baby."

"Thank heavens for that!"

Chapter 48

Damaris Justice let out a big sigh. She was sitting in her kitchen, staring at the laundry basket that Aliseeya had so kindly seen to. Unfortunately, the results just weren't good enough for her exacting standards.

Using her powerful maternal lungs, she bellowed, "Aliseeya, baby! Come down here at once! You folded all dem socks wrong."

"What? Hang on, I'm coming downstairs."

Damaris kissed her teeth.

As soon as Aliseeya appeared, she accosted her mother.

"What's all the fuss about? No wonder Papa used to call you coconut woman. Remember that Harry Belafonte ditty? It went, *Coconut woman is calling out, and every day you can hear her shout.*"

"Stop it with that chupid talk! Let your papa rest in peace, and don't insult your mother."

"Oh, so you can dish it out, but you can't take it, eh? Whatevs. Why on earth did you summon me down here?"

Aliseeya glared at Damaris with a look she normally reserved for Zain when he was being difficult. Damaris bent over from her chair and picked up a balled-up pair of socks, holding it in front of her daughter like evidence from a crime scene.

"And what do you call this, pickney? Wa gwaan witchu? You tink you playing cricket like your fada used to, and you need a ball to trow?"

"Honestly, Mum, even Zain wasn't this much trouble." *God, I miss living with him.* "He did all the washing and folding for both of us."

"That explains it. You never learned how to fold properly. These socks look like you're going to fling them at the wicket!"

Aliseeya kissed her teeth.

"Don't you be making that nasty sound at me, girlie!"

"But it's all right for you to do it, Mommie Dearest?"

"Of caaaars it is, child. I'm from Jamaica. It's a…reflex."

"But it's rude."

"I didn't mean to be rude. I was just expressing my feelings."

"What feelings?"

"I'm vexed."

Aliseeya sat down next to Damaris, exasperated.

"I was only trying to help you, Mum."

"I know."

"I mean, my own life is not exactly tickety-boo right now. Do you realize how hard I had to push Zainy just to take a job? Must you subject me to a tirade about sock rolling?"

"Aliseeya, don't you be rushing that boy into work. You hear what me say?"

"Why must you always take his side?"

"Ain't nobody takin' sides, darlin'. He's the reason you're in London. Praise the Lord. I'm so happy to have you both here. But he's a fragile ting. Zain loves you like no other man's ever gonna love you, so go easy on him. And on these socks, Lorda mercy!"

"All right, this clearly is not about the bloomin' socks. What's really bothering you?"

"It's dat Gulnar." Damaris kissed her teeth with force, causing Aliseeya to raise an eyebrow.

"Oh. Well, I can understand why you're vexed. Auntie Gulnar confounded us all. Poor Zain—my fragile boyfriend of whom you speak—is not even speaking to her, and he lives under her roof. It's all such a shambles."

"I don't blame Gully, exactly. She did what she had to do to get her son back, and I don't be grudging her that."

"Then what's the problem?"

"Now that the foolishness in Tanzania is over, you tink she'd have the decency to pick up the phone and say *boo* to me! I was her best friend. We been like sisters for thirty years, watching you and Zain grow up together. Was saw each other through our husbands' deaths. Why she cyan't put the past behind us?" Damaris made a final, withering kissing noise with her teeth. "Now we are just two lonely widows."

Aliseeya started laughing. "You're not spiders, you know."

"I didn't say black widows."

Aliseeya laughed some more. "I know, but it's pretty funny hearing you use that descriptor."

"Sometimes you're just too clever for your own good, chile. I'm upset about my friendship with Gulnar."

"All right, keep your hair on. What are you going to do about the situation?"

"What rubbish are you talking, Ali baby?"

"Mum, I've traveled everywhere and met some of the brightest, most powerful people. Everyone has disagreements, but no relationship was repaired because someone opined, *If only she would call me.* If you want to make things right with Auntie Gulnar, it's up to *you* to make the first move. You raised me to take action, just like Granny Clarice always used to say."

"I hate it when you're right. All dis time I been thinking that woman, she gone soft in the head. Now I know it was just a show. Well, maybe not entirely. I still tink she's got a few loose screws. But still, she devised quite an elaborate plot just to get poor Zainy the help he needs."

"You should be the bigger person, Damaris."

"Oi, cheeky miss, callin' your mudda by her first name! Who d'you think you're talking to? And are you implying that I'm swaaty?"

Aliseeya laughed again.

"Heavens to Betsy, no, mother dearest. By bigger person, I meant more forgiving."

"Okay, okay. Guh from here, now."

Kissing her teeth as Aliseeya ran back upstairs, Damaris could no longer suppress her smile. *I've got my headstrong girl back, sass and all. Now I just got to put my foolish sister Gulnar right.*

Chapter 49

Damaris appeared at the Jaffars' front door, dressed in her Sunday best at a time when she knew that Zain was out with Aliseeya. She held a floral-decorated tin containing a freshly baked tangerine cake. Nestled in her elbow was a bouquet of white carnations. After pressing the bell with her other elbow, she awaited her fate. *This could all blow up in my face.*

Gulnar opened the door slowly, eyeing Damaris with suspicion.

You're the one who's done me and our kids wrong, and now you have the gall to peer at me like a bobo!

"Oh. Damaris. Hello?"

Keep a civil tongue in your head, Damaris.

"Hello, Gulnar." *She looks chaka-chaka, de poor ting.*

"Darling, it's so nice of you to come 'round. How are you?"

"Look, Gulnar, I'm not here for a social visit. I shan't beat around the bush."

"Very well. Please enlighten me as to your purpose for calling."

"We got to make peace, sister. I know Zain is vex with you. Aliseeya is vex with you. Even I—"

"Good grief, Damaris. If this is how you intend to make peace, you're not exactly a skilled diplomat, are you?"

"You got me there, biscuit."

"Biscuit? My word, I never thought I'd get a compliment out of you."

"You're still a beautiful lady, Gulnar."

"Why, thank you."

Gulnar was wearing a pale-pink blouse and her famous purple skirt with applied seashells—her carapace courage shield.

"Did you know I wore this skirt on the day when there was a mutiny in Dar es Salaam, and I drove myself to school while there were tanks in the streets?"

"Is that so, Gully? What do you think I am, a mumu? You're quite a banton, concocting all these stories, entrapping your own son—"

"Now just you watch it, woman! That really did happen. It was January 20, 1964. You can look it up in the history books if you don't believe me. It's as fresh in my memory as if it were yesterday. And I did meet the first lady of Tanzania, Maria Nyerere."

Damaris resisted the urge to kiss her teeth.

"Well, look it. We're not getting any younger by standing here and rabbiting away."

"You're right about that, of course. But at least I can still fit into the same skirt I wore in 1964."

"Oi! What are you saying? That I'm bufu-bufu?"

"Oh no, darling, I wouldn't dream of it. That comment was all about me. You know how vain I can be."

Finally, the woman has located a shred of self-awareness.

"You should be proud. You kept your maga figure for the more than thirty years that I've known you. Which is why you can eat this tangerine cake I baked especially for you. It won't show."

"Why, thank you, Damaris. How absolutely splendid of you, dear. Won't you come in for a cup of tea?"

"As I said, I'm not here for a social visit. I want you to go and leave this cake on the kitchen counter. Then come back, put on your shoes, and grab one of your silk scarves from the hall cupboard. I'm taking you somewhere special."

"Goody gumdrops. I love a surprise! Where are we going?"

"Woking Cemetery. We're going to visit Anil and Orlando. God rest their souls. Them husbands of ours got off too easy, if you ask me. Leaving us to look after our kids on our own."

Before she knew what she was doing, she kissed her teeth. *I can't help it. It's a reflex.*

"You know dem two. My Aliseeya, always looking for some crazy adventure. And your Zain, facing so many struggles, de poor ting. But he's a good boy, you know."

"I know." Gulnar looked down momentarily. "Listen, Damaris, I feel terrible about—"

"No, no, Gulnar. Cease and sekkle. You see, I can be diplomatic. Let's put all that behind us, shall we? Today, we're thinking about our husbands, letting them know we haven't forgotten them, and asking them to watch over our pickneys."

"Do you know something? I've not been to the graveyard since Anil was buried. I couldn't face it on my own, and Zain wouldn't agree to go anywhere with me. But with you, I have the courage to go."

"You always got me by your side, Gulnar. Just don't try none of that foolishness where you go spinning yarns about Tanzania. Do you hear what me say?"

"Loud and clear. I'm finally ready to put that maelstrom behind me."

"Good. Now let's go celebrate them husbands of ours."

Chapter 50

London, 2012

In the months that followed his return to London, Zain found that the effort of living—getting back into work, locating a flat for Aliseeya and himself (*"As you're currently unemployed, babes, you can find us a place to live."*), and processing all these major life changes—was enough to exhaust him, in a good way.

> *It's better that I should be overwhelmed than bored. An idle mind is my worst enemy.*

He was grateful to have received that nudge from Aliseeya—gentler, by far, than what felt like his mother's attempts to push him over the edge—even if his constant struggle had been how to deal with the feeling of being overwhelmed. He embraced this new life as a better alternative than the sorrowful state he had inhabited for all his years.

Recognizing that his relationship with Aliseeya was the key to his recovery—Zain understood that he could never be rid of his condition, but that loving support could help him—he planned a surprise for her. Even though they were living together in Peckham—in a street far dingier than where they lived in Glasgow—he insisted that she travel alone to meet him at the Malaysian restaurant on Great Windmill Street, where they had officially become a couple.

After traveling from his office at the Tooting London News to run an errand in the West End, he promptly occupied the table he had booked for them, and for their mothers, unbeknownst to Aliseeya. This would be his first time seeing Gulnar since he had moved out of her house.

He had texted his mother about coming to dinner, but otherwise refused to speak to her on the telephone, still taking time to process all that had happened. He was not yet ready to forgive or accept her crazy actions, not just of the past year, but also over the entire period of his relationship with Aliseeya.

Breathe, Zain. Just breathe.

Aliseeya entered, resplendent as ever in her shortly shorn hair, her magnificent stature adorned in a yellow print dress that resembled a cloak, wearing her high heels that inched her close to six-feet tall. Trailing just behind, he spotted Damaris, who always radiated happiness, followed by his own mother, whose face—encrusted with makeup—betrayed no emotion.

Unsurprisingly, Gulnar was dressed to the nines, her still-lithe silhouette framed by a simple white blouse and a pale-green poodle skirt embroidered with roses in various shades of pink. Her wrists bore her ubiquitous gold bangles, and from her earlobes dangled dazzling pink gemstone earrings which shone with blinding brightness, stunning all who beheld her.

Oh, mother, did you have to make this night about you?

As Zain stood up to greet the three most important women in his life, he said, "Hello. What the…you all came together?"

"Hullo, pickney." Damaris smiled while kissing him on the cheek. "When Gulnar and I were chatting the other day, we realized that we would both be attending this dinner, and decided to share a minicab. I don't know what you're up to, but I'm glad you invited me."

"You'll find out in good time, Auntie Damaris, I promise. Did Aliseeya know you were coming to dinner?" *Is my plan falling apart before it's even begun?*

"No, chile. I kept it a secret, like I promised."

"Then how did you happen to arrive with Aliseeya?"

"While we were in the cab, Gulnar spotted Aliseeya walking along Shaftesbury Avenue, so we asked the driver to stop and let her in. None of us know what you've got up your sleeve."

"Damaris is right, Zain. But I know my sneaky son is up to something. Tell me, what's all this in aid of? Making your poor old mum come into town! You know I don't like to cross the river these days."

"You are neither poor nor old, Mother. You certainly weren't old when you were recently traipsing around Dar es Salaam, getting me to chase after you."

"Now, now, Zain, darlin'. Be kind to your mother. She dressed up so nicely for you."

Thank you, Auntie Damaris, peacekeeper.

"Very well. You lot will see what I'm up to in due course. Please, ladies, do sit down. Ali, you come here next to me. And Mum and Aunty Damaris, you can be opposite us."

"Hmph. Not even a phone call for months, and now this keeping us in the dark?"

You just can't help yourself, can you, Mother? This night is not about you.

"Please, Auntie Gulnar, can we keep the peace for just one evening? I love this place. It holds special memories for Zain and me."

"That, it does. Speaking of which…" *Breathe, Zain. Just breathe.*

The women had learned to be patient with Zain as he negotiated his way through conversations. A task that would seem straightforward to most was arduous for him. Tonight, he felt as though he had a mountain to climb. Which was why he had wanted the support of their mothers, even if it meant facing Gulnar.

Just breathe. Come on, Zain, you can do it.

"Well, ladies, here it is—the reason I've asked you all here tonight. Here it is…"

His heart was pounding—*tick, tick, tick.*

"Aliseeya, will you marry me?"

All three women gasped in a chorus of exuberance.

Aliseeya nodded and smiled, tears streaking down her face. With a stunned expression, she examined the ring he held out in his palm, which bore a gleaming blue tanzanite stone.

Damaris who broke the silence. "Congratulations to you both! Zain, darling, I'm chuffed to bits that you've asked my Ali to marry you. May the two of you be very happy. I've always thought of you as my son. Now you can finally call me mum."

"Thank you, Missus Justice."

"No need to be that formal, dear."

"Very well, Auntie Damaris. I'll hold off on calling you mum until after the wedding. We don't want any bad luck."

"Fair enough, sugar." Damaris elbowed Gulnar.

Subtle.

"Congratulations, Aliseeya dear. Welcome to the family."

And then Aliseeya came out with something truly stunning.

"Thank you, Auntie Gulnar. You know as well as I do that this doesn't mean anything without your blessing. Now, will the two of you please kiss and makeup? Zain, go and hug your mother."

I know when I'm defeated.

He stood and sheepishly approached the glamorous Gulnar, who had to straighten her ornamental skirt from puffing out as she stood awkwardly to return his embrace.

While the two were hugging—at first reticently, then slowly warming into a proper mother-child hug—she whispered, "I'm so proud of you, darling."

"Thanks."

"Your dad would be, too. You've turned out to be the man he always wanted you to be."

"I-I-I know."

Still embracing her son, she said, "Um, there's one more thing, Zainy."

"What is it, Mum?"

"I'm sorry."

"I-I-I know."

As the two returned to their seats, Gulnar dabbed at her eyes with a lace handkerchief.

"Right," she said. "Now that my heart is back in my chest, shall we have a toast?"

"Yes, let's do." Aliseeya was still beaming.

"To the happy couple," said Damaris.

"To the happy couple," Gulnar added.

Aliseeya and Zain clinked their glasses together and beheld each other with a look of pure happiness, not in some abstract, imaginary future, but just as they were at this very moment.

Having overcome his natural reticence, Zain said, "I, for one, am over the moon."

Beaming, he observed these three beautiful women—his fiancée, his future mother-in-law, and even his own mother, begrudgingly.

"And it bears saying that I am an incredibly lucky man."

"That, you are." Aliseeya gripped his hand.

Acknowledgments

This novel wouldn't have been written without three departed souls whose light shines forever: my father Mohamed Vellani, my aunt Sheema Parsons, and my best friend Bruce Mastalinski. They believed in me before I believed in myself. I do not mourn them; they reside within me.

I owe an enormous debt of gratitude to my first reader John Wall Barger, who quickly made the transition from literary friend to brother after a fortuitous Valentine's Day meeting at the Kelly Writers House. To my Penn Writing family: Val Ross, Al Filreis, Sara Byala, Mingo Reynolds, R.J. Bernocco, Jamie-Lee Josselyn, Jim Grilli, Matthew Osborn, Jake Rutkowski, Patrick Wehner, and Rodger LeGrand.

To my cousin Alia Pirani, for reading my earliest forays into fiction and shepherding my literary and musical dreams as if they were her own. To my cousins Altaaf Hasham, Alyssa Hasham, Aziz Rajwani, Bashir Hasham, Emilie Blanc, Feisel Haji, Latif Hasham, Sabrina Hasham, Sophia Loques, Yasmin Visram, and Zarina Rajwani, for your unstinting support.

To the writers who told me - emphatically - that I could write this novel: Sikeena Ahmed Karmali, Farah Ahamed, Vikram Paralkar, Nate Walker, John Ghazvinian, Mathangi Subramanian, Manel Guitart, Robert Kohls, Ru Freeman, Joe Hustko, Farid Azfar, Zahid Chaudury, Aptin Khanbaghi, Kamila Shamsie, Nadeem Aslam, M.G. Vassanji, Ghalib Shiraz Dhalla, Shinho Lee, Ian Iqbal Rashid, Gurinder Chadha.

To my cousin Saleema Vellani, who has walked the author's journey alongside me. To my cousin Tazeem Moledina, who has nurtured my artistic spirit. To my cousin Adil Vellani, without whom I would have no confidence. To Riaz, Dinar, and Aman Vellani, for always encouraging me. To the heads of our family, Firoz and Naseem Vellani, for your belief in me. To all my relatives: The Alanis, Blancs, Dayas, Hajis, Hashams, Ladha Kassams, Lams, Manjis, Merchants, Moledinas, Rashids, Rajwanis, Somers, Sonawallas, Talaksis, Vellanis, and Visrams. Because of each one of you, the love we share as a family has found its way onto these pages. To my childhood friend and the nurturer of my dreams, Salima Kheraj. To my friend Zulfikar Gulamhusein, who insisted I become the artist he always believed I could be. To my sister Lisa Lewis, who encouraged me to write this novel when it was but a twinkle in my eye. To my soul siblings Jamie Watkins and Jatinder Singh, who dance alongside me every step of the way.

To my London family who have adopted and supported me throughout my literary journey: Shaheen, Zahara, Ruhi, Jian, and Kais Andany. I love Ruhi, Jian and Kais as if they were my own, as I love my godson Noah Ahmed.

To my New York family, who have held my hand through the ordeals and celebrated my joys: Gustav Sigurdsson, Thomas Ahn, Farah Alani, Alnoor Maherali, Steve Edwin, and David Fobair. This novel - and my life as we know it - would not be possible without you.

To my Hill College House family for making my home a place in which I have thrived: Julie Sochalski and Bob Cwiklik, Stephanie and Derric Turner, Elizabeth and Robert Scheyder, Valerie Houck, Barbara Jackson, and all the Resident Assistants, members of staff, and students who make this community so special.

To Shaun Carson, for not letting me give up when publishing seemed an unreachable dream. To my Waterloo friends who embraced me from day one: Allen Clark, Drew Clark, Mark Tabur, and Paul Clarke. To Manish Mehta, who has nourished my soul from our very first meeting.

To Murray Savar, whom I am fortunate to count as part of my logical family. To Byron Lee, a kindred spirit and fellow lover of all things shiny and dazzling. To Henri David, a riveting storyteller, true friend, and the enabler of my love affair with all things shiny and dazzling!

To Anita Wang, who had faith in me at my lowest ebb, and with whom I have shared some of the deepest belly-aching laughs. To Peter Campbell, who helped make London my home again. To Emmanuelle Dirix, with whom I ate two lunches on that fateful day in Camden Town.

To Faraan Mithani, who inspired me to climb Mount Kilimanjaro, cementing my love for Tanzania and sparking a desire to write this novel. To Naveed Nanjee, who bought me a diary for that Kilimanjaro trip; I wrote my earliest fiction in that diary. To Omar Khoury, a true inspiration from day one.

To the relatives who have housed, supported, and nurtured me: Mohamed and Almas Daya, Rahima Alani, Nazim and Sujatha Rashid, Zul and Shahzia Daya, Fidu and Nurjehan Moledina, Yasmin and Mehboob Kanji, Roshan and Shenie Dhanji, Zainab and Abdulaziz Moledina, Zarina Rajwani, Moaiz and Nurjehan Daya, Sabrina Hasham, Gulzar Raisa Charania, Aziz Rajwani, Zarin and François Blanc, Sophia and José Loques, Emilie Blanc and Jerome Gattini.

To my band mates in Khayal - a musical family that has cultivated my creativity - Zaeem, Farah, Feizin, Daya, Shamji, Faisal, Arif, Prithpal, Skelly.

To my friends who have supported me with love and encouragement: Aalia Datoo, Al-Riaz Adatia, Alasdair Pinkerton, Alan Dolan, Alexander Gray, Alif Dharamsi, Allyson Boodle, Alvin Hall, Amaan Ismail, Andy Curd, Antonio Galan, Ayeesha Sachedina, Aziz Boghani, Aziz Esmail, Becky Stephens and Katrina Glanzer, Bonnie and Peter Stephens, Brad Thomas, Carlando Francis, Carlos Vega, Carol and George Bevan, Celia Rodrigues, Chris Silva, Dan Murphy, Daniel Swingley, David Tompkins, Demo Gakidis, Diane and Julia Gordon, Dipal Shah and Landon Ewers, Duncan Sones, Eleve Zelenak and Travis Sloane, Emilia McKee-Vasallo, Eric Speers, Farahana Jaffer, Farahana Jaffer, Fatima Dhanani, Firoz, Juby and Naz Bhagad, Florian Scheding, Hariprasad Kowtha, Heather Durham, Helen Gilks and Tim Copestake, Helga Haack, Iñaki Muñoz, Insiyah Jamal, Jamey Rorison, Jamie Rae, Jann Klose, Jared Susco and Chris Stearns, Jason Nguyen, Jefferson Darrell, Jo-Ann Forslund, Joe Cheng and Andrew Pinto, Joe Kerr, Johnny Antoun, Jordan Wellwood, Jordane Jolley, Jordi Rovira, Joy and Howie Strech, Karim Hassam Bhagad, Karim H. Karim, Karim Ladak, Kevin Bailey and Ludger Viefhuis, Kevin Henry, Luis Madrid, Luther Obrock, Marian Moravek, Matthew Holdsworth, Michael Short, Mike Mani, Moyez Alwani, Nada Drozd, Naseem Jivraj, Neil Ghosh, Neil Guthrie, Niel DuPreez, Nurbanu Akbarali, Nurjehan Vassanji, Paul Mills, Paulette Hamilton, Pearce Groover, Pierre Gaudibert, Rahim Eboo, Ray McKenna, Richard Andrews, Ricky Gresh, Rob Imrie, Rubina Jasani, Ryan Keytack, Ruben Luna, Sabila Eboo, Sandie and Daniel Mattioli, Sahil Warsi, Selina Kassam Ramji, Shainila Pradhan, Shaleen Hudda Mulvaney, Shawna Lurie, Sherin Manji, Soraiya Kara, Soraiya Verjee, Stuart Bustard, Sylvia White, Tim Jivaranuntakul, Tom Gilks, Tom Oxenham, Todd Smith-Bergollo, Travis Bose, Winnie Allingham, Whitney Rolle, and Yi-Lin Tsai.

To my publisher Kassahun Checole, thank you for believing in this novel and giving it a voice. To my editor Girma Demeke, you have been a joy to work with. To the entire team at Africa World Press and Red Sea Press, thank you for producing such a beautiful publication.

To my soon to be brother-in-law and fellow author Daniel Zimberoff, thank you for your friendship, support, and legal advice.

To Kate Kramer, who shares not just an office with me, but also a vision for this book, helping me bring it into fruition.

To Lisa Brown, a new friend I have known in a previous lifetime, who has become my champion on this literary journey.

To the talented Tavia Nyong'o, for your many kindnesses since our early days at Yale, and for painting a stunningly gorgeous image to adorn the novel's cover. I am in awe of your artistry.

Finally, I want to thank my beloved John for all that you have done to nurture and support me. Your encouraging me to write during our honeymoon - and giving me time and space to do so - helped me see this novel to completion. Your love is a blessing I cherish forever.